THE

CRAWFORD COUNTY

◆ SKETCHBOOK ◆

THE
CRAWFORD
COUNTY
SKETCHBOOK

Domine, non sum dignus

◆ ◆ ◆

TOM JANIKOWSKI

RED HEN PRESS | PASADENA, CA

Book design and layout by Mark E. Cull

Library of Congress Cataloging-in-Publication Data
Janikowski, Tom, 1968–
  The Crawford County Sketchbook / Tom Janikowski.—First edition.
    pages cm
  ISBN 978-1-59709-533-4 (pbk. : alk. paper)
  I. Title.
  PS3610.A5693C84 2015
  813'.6—dc23
                        2015006430

The Los Angeles County Arts Commission, the National Endowment
for the Arts, the Pasadena Arts & Culture Commission and the City of
Pasadena Cultural Affairs Division, Sony Pictures Entertainment, the
Los Angeles Department of Cultural Affairs, the Dwight Stuart Youth
Fund, and the Ahmanson Foundation partially support Red Hen Press.

First Edition
Published by Red Hen Press
www.redhen.org

For Shelly, my one and only love

5-21

CONTENTS

THE

CRAWFORD COUNTY
◆ SKETCHBOOK ◆

PART I

The Crawford County Sketchbook

HAVERLAND—MR. PETER SWITCHBACK, Jr., 43, of rural Crawford County, died at 11:51 a.m. Monday, July 12.

He was born in Haverland to Peter Switchback and Ruth Mae Blair Switchback, and is survived by a brother, David, of Pole Creek.

He was preceded in death by a sister, Lily.

Peter proudly served eight years in the U.S. Navy on several ships and coastal installations and was most recently self-employed as a writer and consultant and maintained his family's plantation and estate.

He was a life-long Christian and attended St. Alban's Anglican Church in Cotton City, although he charitably supported all of the churches of Crawford County.

Funeral services will be at 2 p.m. Thursday, July 15, at St. Alban's Anglican Church with Father Michael Stencil officiating. There will be no visitation. Burial will be in Memorial Park Cemetery. Military honors will be provided by the Custis Hewitt American Legion Post 285.

Memorials may be made to the St. Alban's Endowment Fund, the Guild of Mary, or to a charity of the donor's choice.

Prelude

I

If the rocks in this place could talk, they'd tell you to ask the trees. If the trees in this place could talk, they'd tell you to ask the wind. And if the wind could talk, hell, it would tell you that this place has no soul. Then the wind would ask you just what it is that you expected, as if you might think that a place would ever have any kind of a soul.

The wind has blown over this place since there has been something that people chose to call "wind," or since there has been such a thing as a place, and no one is quite sure which of those two came first. We once heard a theologian say that the wind came first, for it was the very breath of God that swept over this place and made it holy, for the ground is holy. We knew he was a theologian, you see, because he had a long, white beard and he got to speaking of holy things.

When the wind dies down you might find out that this place has sold all that it ever had—that if there was anything at all to be had here then the whole place would have sold its birthright for a bowl of grits. Some days there isn't even that bowl of grits to fall back on and the soul of this place just goes to bed hungry, and a hungry soul is a sad thing—useful only to preachers and used car salesmen and folks who want to strike a deal for something they know they can't back up. Maybe sometimes those are all the same thing. But then, maybe this place has never been big on wisdom—just on living.

They call it Crawford County on the maps, and it is Crawford County on our tongues and it is home in our hearts—hearts that have watched over and struggled and grieved and mourned this place and her long shadows and a heart like an empty bowl of grits. Yankee peddlers came first, then Appalachian dirt farmers. No one really remembers who the first ones were, but everyone knows the last, for it was the person doing the remembering, naturally, and it was up to the one doing the remembering to be the one doing the grieving, as well. As if you could grieve what you never had and what a whole, painful beating heart full of generations never had. It just cannot be done, and I would challenge anyone to prove otherwise.

Maybe you had best pour yourself a dark cup of coffee if you are reading this in the morning time or a nice, cold sweet tea if it is the afternoon. If it is the evening, you would be at your liberty to pour yourself a short glass of bourbon that someone brought down from some place up in Kentucky, but I best warn you that Crawford County is a dry county and they have themselves a sheriff that might not cotton to whiskey being drunk in the vicinity. Consider yourself warned, leastaways.

If the sun gets too hot, it's best to take off your hat and stand in the middle of the yard or to step out in the middle of a pea field and look up at that fiery ball in the sky. Curse at it. Throw a handful of that sacred soil up into the sky and let it fall like manna from Heaven. It might never return to the earth, in fact, just as the word of God is said to never return to his mouth empty. The soil would go to a different place, though, just as the hearts and the minds and the souls of our kinfolk and neighbors go to a different place—they go one place while they are living and breathing and thinking of a life they haven't got and a life they wish they had and the blessed yet stale reality of the life they have been dealt, and they go to a different place entirely when the day is done and the cold potted meat is put on a plate along with greens, if you're lucky.

The Lord giveth and the earth and the sky and the wind and the rain and the coldest of hearts taketh away; blessed be the Name of the Lord. And blessed be the earth and the sky and the wind and the rain, for they take what we do not have and what we do not deserve and if we are lucky they might return a blessing on account of what we have done. Cursed be the coldest of hearts, however— they just take and they take and they take. Cursed be the coldest of hearts, for they just never know that what they take is something that leaves the other impoverished and kicking around that dusty old pea field, listening to cicadas, feeling the sweaty scratch of their dirty shirt and wishing for a cup of cool water.

Oh, you might stare and you might snicker and turn away. You might be one of those "snickering idiots" like my darling wife calls them. You might just shake your head and go on home to a nice piece of chicken-fried steak, and I really wouldn't blame you if you did, for I purely love chicken-fried steak. I do love fried chicken more, but sometimes in Crawford County you can only get barbecue and sweet tea, so I guess you'll take what you can get. And I wouldn't blame you, like I said. Just make sure that you know that by turning away from some of those folks in that once-idyllic and now dusty and forlorn corner of a forgotten, abandoned, and defeated expanse of God's creation you really turn away from yourself. You turn away, we all turn away. We are really not all that different, and the same folks are inside of us all. Folks are folks, and that doesn't ever change.

II

There's good in some folks that would outshine the evil in others and then there's evil in some that seems to totally out-darken the brightest shining lights. We got both kinds here in Crawford County, but then I suppose that they have those kinds anywhere you go. The dark ones always seem to be darkest when you stand them up against or next to some of the bright ones. Have you noticed that? Well, take the folks here in Crawford County, for an instance. You take the best men and women that we got and you stick them in a room, maybe sitting on a bench or a sofa or on something just relaxing and being kind of easy-going, and then you go and grab yourself the worst men and women in Crawford County and stick them in the same room, on the same bench or such, and I guarantee you are going to see the difference beyond your wildest imagination. The good looks better and the bad looks worse when it is standing next to that which it ain't. It doesn't take some kind of genius to reckon that, though, I suppose.

Maybe it's in the water, or maybe it's in the air, or maybe it's in the breeding and the living of the families in this county, but it just ends up that there are certain families that have a knack for turning out real demons and others that have a way of turning out saints. Some say that if times had been different then the families might be different, but that's just speculation, I suppose. It is what it is, and they are what they are. Time could maybe change things, but I ain't going to hold my breath waiting on it.

In the middle of summer, sometimes, you can look out over one of those blessed pea fields and look for about as long as you can see— about as long as you might want to look, and you might even see as far as God Almighty himself would ever want a person to see. More to the point, if you just look out at the horizon and you let your heart see what is there but your eyes can't see, then you might just see the most important things of all, and you might just get to the point where you care about them. Then again, you might take the heart of the other half of the folks 'round here and just think that the dry, dusty old pea fields hold only sadness and hard work of the sort that makes you a broken man by the time you aren't very old at all. But go ahead and look, and find out if you just can't see something that doesn't seem to be there. It's there, all right. It's there.

When the night comes, and that stillness comes down upon the land kind of like a big old blanket of the sort your grandmother or your mother or your great-aunt might have made in a time before the time when everyone was buying their blankets at some big old store in Cotton City, well, when that time comes, you might want to go and take a look again in the very same place, and see if those ghosts come out to play. I ain't saying that this place is haunted—not in the typical way, mind you; I ain't saying that at all—it just seems that the fears and the sadness and the lost dreams and all of the hopes that got ground down to nothing in a dry old pea field just sort of hang around for a while, and if you listen real close, you can hear that field weepin'. It seems to be a weepin', but sometimes it's more like a moan if the wind is right. Maybe it is just the wind. But remember what I told you earlier—if you could ask the wind, then it would tell you this place has no soul, but then the wind would ask you what you expected, as if you might think that a place would have a soul.

III

You'll see. There's a lot to be had here, but then there's always been a lot to lose, as well, and most people have come up on the losin' side if they thought they were gonna make themselves rich. It was mostly those who start out trying to live honestly rather than high on the hog, as it were, who come out doing OK. I think that they are really the ones who find that one might do just fine in this county.

Just the other day an old man sat down next to me at the diner and said, "The Good Lord made Adam and Eve, but I don't think he saw the rest of it coming." I begged to differ with him, as I figured that the Good Lord pretty much had a handle on everything that was going to happen . . . in fact, I don't think that we really surprise him all that much. Maybe we disappoint him quite a bit every now and then, but we sure don't surprise him. It was kind of like old Doc MacFadden said to me when I had to tell him about that problem I had with the water. I told him that I felt bad tellin' him, but he said, "Hell, you can't really surprise me with much, you know. I've pretty much seen it all." I told him all about it after that, and now I've told all of you who are readin' this, so I guess I must be pretty much over the embarrassment. Or maybe it was shame. What is the difference, anyway? I don't know.

Well, when it comes down to surprising folks, it sure is a far sight easier to surprise a sheriff or a store clerk or a farmer than it is to surprise Almighty God. I guess you know that, and I sure don't have to tell you, but it bears repeating, anyway. You'll come to notice this and believe it if you go hanging around these parts long enough, and you might even come to appreciate it, especially after you've been surprised yourself a few times. There comes a point, though, where even a body or a part of a body or someone crying when they should be laughing or a lost child covered in some kind of paint or a cow that got all turned inside out won't surprise you as much as it used to. When my cousin Todd's arm got caught in that one piece of machinery on the farm, it was bad. But as the machine kept spinning for a bit, we saw his hand on the end of his arm go whippin' by a few times, slowin' down as it went. It looked for all the world like his arm and his hand were waving at us, so my cousin Lyle started waving back at it, saying, "How you doin', Todd? Howdy there Todd!" Todd was rolling on the ground screaming and bleeding everywhere, but Lyle was laughing himself until he nearly got sick. No, it wasn't funny, but it was just what I expected, in a way, and I sure got no kind of surprise out of it. Todd was really the only one who was surprised. Hell of a way to get a surprise. He was OK, though. We called him Lefty after that, and he didn't mind. Not at all.

So surprising Almighty God is going to be pretty hard, and I ain't all that sure you ever can quite get the job done. When God Almighty takes a good hard look at this here county, I get the distinct feeling that he sees right through all the dust and the squinty-eyed ignoring that other folk put on so they don't have to own up to the truth. But Almighty God, he probably sees right through it and he cares. Yes, sir, I believe he does.

The County is a hot one, but the heart of The County can be a cold one and the man who was selling chicken livers and chicken gizzards and chicken hearts out of a big, shiny metal box out back of the filling station said this thing about cold hearts and how they are so much different than the gizzards and the livers. He said that the hearts, when they get cold, they taste different, and not nearly as good as a cold liver. 'Cause, Hell, my aunt Elizabeth used to make this dish with cold chicken livers and it was pretty good. I can't really speak for the gizzards, 'cause I ain't never eaten a cold gizzard, so that leaves the hearts, and I will just go and take it on the authority of the man behind the filling station that the hearts just don't hold up as well when they get cold. They get cold and tough and hard to deal with and you just don't want to have to deal with a heart that done grown cold.

Chicken or otherwise.

Spirit Spring

Daddy was a flagpole sitter and Momma raised chickens for the state. That is, she grew them chickens for the man at the college, and he took them chickens when he needed them. Daddy didn't ever make no money sittin' on flagpoles, but he sure got a good name for it all over the county, and it helped him find men who were suckers enough to help fund his outlandish schemes. Schemes like you never would believe, no how. Daddy once said he was gonna find a way to dig hisself an underground complex of roads that went so far in a wild-ass maze and at the end he was gonna set up shop as a liquor store and beat The County blue laws. He figured that if it were far enough an underground walk to the store then there was no way anyone would think it was on county land and then they couldn't stop him from sellin' whiskey. Damn fool flagpole sitter.

We all commenced to helpin' Daddy dig on a fine day when the skies looked like they still had a little hope left in 'em. We all grabbed shovels and Daddy had what he called a "mattock." He'd be swingin' that thing and lookin' half-crazed. What does "whole-crazed" mean, anyway? You never hear anyone say "whole-crazed" and I kinda wished you did, 'cause it would be a good way of talkin' 'bout a lot of folks I know.

Daddy had that shaft dug down maybe twenty feet and then over toward the neighbor's farm maybe thirty feet or so, and he came down sick. The shaft looked pretty good, and me and my friends used to sit and look down into it and wait to see if anything ever came out. Dan Boyle from down the road said there would be some kind of insects that would creep out of such a deep hole over nights, maybe, but I didn't ever see anything come out of that hole. Daddy never went back down into it, no how.

Daddy woke up that mornin' saying that he just woke up old. He had a cold or a pain that settled down in his back and he started coughing a lot. We never knew what it was, and Doctor MacFadden never really knew either. The Doctor actually said that he thought it was like my daddy said—that he just done woke up old one morning. Momma died that next spring and we kids had to find jobs to help keep things goin'. We tried keeping up the chickens, but weren't too good at it. Most of the chickens died and that hen house got to smellin' pretty bad, seein' as how we were all afraid to go in and gather up all the dead ones. That prob'ly wasn't too bright, but what're you gonna do? By fall we sold the farm and Daddy went and lived in that thing Uncle Rod called the pension house. Daddy died the next year from something that we never heard of before. Doctor MacFadden told us what it was, but I didn't pay no mind—I just figured it had to do with Daddy waking up old that one day.

After they was all gone, I kinda' got to driftin'. I never did finish school, and I found it more fun to move from town to town and take odd jobs here and there. I never did no flagpole-sittin', 'cause I figured there was no money in it, just like Daddy had found out, but I did do some building climbing—mostly to wash windows and such. I always wished that I had learned how to sit on those flag-poles, as kind of a tribute to Daddy, but I never did. Life gets like that, you know—wishin' to do something and then you wake up one day and you're old so you never get around to learnin' how to sit on a flagpole or dig yourself an underground liquor store. All those hopes and dreams sometimes they just go away and maybe even end up smellin' a little bit—hopes and dreams that die and start to smell maybe just a little bit sweet, yet. Hopes and dreams that smell like those dead chickens in the hen house—dead chickens that you find yourself a little too scared to grab, 'cause you just don't like touchin' things that are dead. Seems so unnatural, somehow.

Unnatural isn't such a bad thing, but when things are dead, that seems so much more than just unnatural, and when they s'posed to be livin' all the while you find 'em dead, that's even worse. But when a man has his dreams and the dreams give him life and then the dreams they end up dyin' but the man goes on livin', well, maybe that's just the most unnatural thing of all. Even more unnatural than a dead chicken that you don't wanna touch and that when you do you think that as soon as you can you just gotta get back in the house and wash the dead offa your hands. The dead and the unnatural part of a man losin' his dreams, though, that part you just can't wash off with simple soap and water. So like I said, sometimes a man just wakes up old.

Barrels Found in Field

by Respite Welk of the Crawford County Recorder

Four empty barrels that had previously contained a potentially explosive substance were found Friday morning in a field owned by Mr. Cletus Ford of Owen Township, according to Crawford County Sheriff Cecil Morgan. The barrels appear to have been abandoned empty, giving rise to questions concerning the whereabouts of the chemical.

Mr. Ford noticed the empty barrels while working behind his chicken coop and, after inspecting the barrels himself, decided to call the authorities. "I thought maybe they'd have something in them," said Mr. Ford. "I was hoping for some liquor or maybe pesticide, but I don't got that kind of luck."

Sheriff Morgan has said that he will conduct a thorough investigation throughout the county in hope of finding the source of the barrels as well as the person or persons responsible for discarding the barrels on private property. "This kind of damned shenanigan is a Class 3 misdemeanor, and I'm gonna nail the [expletive deleted] who done it," said Sheriff Morgan in a prepared statement this afternoon.

Anyone with information regarding the barrels should contact Crawford County Sheriff Cecil Morgan immediately.

In a Tiny Little Tin

Sicily Preston. Her daddy done rode and fought in the Big One and he went to a place called Sicily and that was why he named his daughter that. Sicily. A pretty name for a pretty girl—and I don't know about that place in Italy that she's named after, but I wonder if it came out kind of the same and I imagine maybe Sicily does sometime, too. Sicily the girl, not Sicily the place in Italy where her daddy fought.

Sicily Preston. That family of hers been 'round here a long time, and her great- or great-great-granddad or some such noise rode with General Stuart in the other war. They was horsemen, all, and that kind of stuck around in the Preston family. That ain't really important to the story of Sicily Preston, I s'pose, but it gives a wonderful color to the story of that blond-haired beauty—for you can almost imagine her long blond mane flowin' like a plume in General Stuart's hat and there ain't a boy alive in Crawford County who would be tellin' the truth if they said that they ain't thought about riding something when they think of Sicily Preston—and yeah, I mean that in the way you think. Yeah, you know I do. She set more men's hearts to pumpin' and more men's privates frankly to swellin' than any other girl I know of. Yeah, you heard what I said. Your momma told you all about that sort of thing, didn't she? Yeah, I thought so.

So Sicily Preston, she got them hearts to thumpin' and when she would drape her long, long legs over the edge of the sideways-fallen tree down at the swimmin' hole, all the guys would look and stare, and some would even get thoughts, I have no doubt. Tyler Hoakum, that one time when he got a little too worked up over something (and I think it was quite likely Sicily's long bare legs hangin' over the edge of that tree), he ended up stayin' all crouched down in pretty shallow water, all the while turnin' red and shakin'. Pilly Straite went swimmin' underwater to see what Tyler was doin' and when he splashed up to the surface he shouted at the top of his lungs, "Tyler's got a chubbie! Tyler's got a chubbie!" Everyone laughed real hard—almost to the point of snortin', and it looked like Sicily knew that Tyler had been starin' at those long, long legs of hers, so she just got real uncomfortable for a minute, and got down off the tree. She walked to the shore and wrapped a towel around herself, but the damage had already been done. Tyler was scarred and picked up the nickname "Chubbie," even though he was always pretty skinny. Damn Pilly.

Years later, Chubbie used to sit around this one dark, dirty bar in Cotton City most of the day and almost every day. He'd sit there and be real quiet, especially if anyone he knew from home would show up, which wasn't really all that often, seein' as how most folk from the county stayed outta Cotton City whenever they could help it—'ceptin' for a doctor exam or buyin' a big appliance or go-ing to the pawn shop or seein' that one proctologist. Some went for that. He's real gentle, with thin fingers.

Chubbie would drink a lot some days. Some days he wouldn't drink so much. A lot of days he would just be real quiet, and if you asked me I would say that he looked like he had a headache of some sort—one of those real thumpers that takes over a whole part of your head and makes you want to drive an ice pick in there or some-thing, just to make it stop. If ever a young woman came into that place, and if ever that young woman was wearin' a short skirt, and if ever she sat where Chubbie could see her, well, Chubbie would up and leave in a huff and lookin' all nauseous and such. Poor guy, he never met a woman he could talk to ever since that day at the swimmin' hole, and it seemed as though girls only made him kinda uncomfortable. But those who knew him way long ago, well we could all tell you that he had been a pretty normal kid, and he never really had a problem talking to girls before, but you know that's how something can mark someone. That reminds me of Ricky Milton. You want to hear about him? Maybe you remember him.

Ricky Milton was a pretty normal kid, really, even though he was a little "whippy" as my aunt Elizabeth used to call it. He was a little high-energy and was just a bit of a homebody. Back when there were different meanings for words—you know, "crack" was a break and "coke" was a drink and "hoe" was a thing you used in a garden—God, how I miss those days. Well, in those days the word "gay" just meant happy for most folk, even though for some it meant something else and some people just ain't too bright. Well, some of the kids at the public school heard the word "gay" on a TV show referring to something else, and before the term had any other meaning in these parts, these kids asked poor little Ricky Milton one day if he was gay. Ricky, hell, he just knew it meant happy, and even though he thought this was a strange question, he just said, "Sure, of course I'm gay." The kids made no end of fun of him, 'cause a whole bunch were in on the joke, as they saw it, and Ricky warn't. It was a bad week for Ricky at school and I think the rest of that year was pretty bad as well, as you know how kids are. It was back before any kind of political correctness, back in the 1970s, and teachers just didn't care, didn't care even if they woulda' heard something that sounded outta line. Ricky just took it and took it inside to himself, and it sat in there, and it festered, and hell, no, he warn't gay like you think nowadays, and Ricky just really knew the kids were makin' fun of him and he really had no way of controlling the situation that had spun out of control for him. Damn. Poor kid.

A lot of the kids who ended up coming to his funeral never dreamt when they started pokin' at him that they were pokin' a pretty big hole. It was in his senior year and he just couldn't take it no more. We don't have a lot of suicides here in Crawford County, as most of what might be suicides really end up lookin' a hell of a lot like farm accidents and no one except really close friends and family are any the wiser. Ricky was different in that way. When a kid shoots himself in a locked school van right outside of the school building, you kinda get the idea that it really wasn't foul play.

It wasn't foul play, but I s'pose you'd be hard pressed to explain that to Ricky Milton. Kinda hard to tell Tyler Hoakum that there was no kinda foul play in his case either, but then, pain and death and foul play sometimes take lots of different shapes.

A Past Master

If you sit down right there I think I could tell you a thing or two about that pus-jacketed flat-foot they call Cecil Morgan. Yeah, he's been the sheriff of Crawford County goin' on twelve years now, but if you want the truth, he ain't nothin' more than a bad guy tryin' to look like a good guy. Ain't never been more than that, no how.

Sid—that's what we called him growin' up—he used to piss everyone off in school, but he met his match in Silas Tilley. Silas pissed off even his own ma, I bet. Silas had a hunchback, and this left eye that kinda popped outta his head, and he used to carry a tube of bright red lipstick with him ever'where he went. He'd put the lipstick on his thumb and the joint of his index finger, walk up to folks and pinch 'em on the cheek, shoutin' out in a high, squeaky voice, "Pinchy pinchy!" That would leave a lipstick kiss mark on their cheek and it would leave 'em pissed off at Silas. He would do this in the hallways in high school, he done it in the hog plant where he got a job after school, and so far as I know it, he done it right up to the point where someone done bashed his skull right in with a broken old paver from the brick kiln out by the river. You know the place, and if you don't you will, 'cause damned near ever'one in Crawford County gets around to gettin' out there. Curiosity killed the cat, they say, and a brick in the head killed Silas Tilley, so far as I can tell.

Dang. That damned Tilley came waltzin' out to the edge of town one hot summer day where ever'one was swimmin' in the river and throwin' rocks into the ruins of the brick kiln, and Sid was playin' around with Dahlia Murphee (yessir, that would be the Colonel's daughter and the future Mrs. Morgan). He was sweet on her and, even though he was fully clothed he was liftin' her up on his shoulders and walkin' around in the river. They was gettin' to chicken fights and laughin' and cuttin' up and such and just havin' a perfect summer afternoon. That's just when Tilley came waltzin' down to the riverbank and waded right into the water in his bloody, crap-smeared overalls from the hog plant. The hunchback and that popped-out eye and that crazy, yellow- and brown-toothed grin . . . near' ever'one stopped what they was doin' and they stared at that Silas Tilley who just turned and walked along the bank, waist-deep in the river. He was sayin' something. Some said it sounded like he was singin' a dirge or a sad hymn such as he learned in Sunday school. I don't know. He just walked downriver with that popped-out eye flittin' back and forth and those lips wobblin' like they was pale red pork fat.

A little while later, when near' ever'one had forgot Silas Tilley had been there, he seemed to just show up again, and there he was lookin' at the backside of Dahlia Murphee who was standin' calf-deep in the water, talkin' to Pandora Hemmingham. Ol' bastard Tilley had greased up his thumb and index finger joint with a nice coat of that bright red lipstick, and he reached down and pinched the very bottom of her bare left buttock for all he was worth, making a kissing sound with his lips and then shoutin', "Pinchy pinchy!" as Dahlia cried out in pain, shock, and horror. You woulda' thought she had been stabbed through the heart, or maybe somewhere else, but she flopped down in the shallow water on her hands and knees and was cryin' and carryin' on and holdin' on to her bottom.

When old Sid heard the screamin' from Dahlia and the shoutin' from Silas Tilley, he turned around right quick. He looks over at Dahlia and all he can see is her holdin' on to her left butt cheek and a big old smear of bright red that he took to be blood but was really only that bright red lipstick from Tilley's hand. Cecil Morgan, he went all wild, I mean to tell you. Old Sid flew into a rage and dove at Silas Tilley and pulled the guy outta the water and hauled him up into the ruins of the brick kiln and we all heard shoutin' and punchin' and more shoutin' and damn near ever'one left. We all ran outta there and just headed back to the gravel road headin' toward the village and back toward Cotton City, seein' as there were some folks from Cotton City there that day.

When we were all back to the fillin' station, drinkin' RC Colas and shakin' from wonderin' what went on, well, Hell, there shows up Cecil Morgan, all drippin' wet and white and shakin' himself. Sid told us that Silas Tilley crapped himself and ran home, as Sid told him he would whup his ass if he ever let that happen again. We thought Silas prob'ly got off pretty easy if that was all that Sid done to him, but we wasn't none too sure about what had gone on anyway.

The next week, after Silas hadn't been seen for a few days, some folk went out lookin' for him and they found his bloated, hunch-backed body face down on a brick pile not too far from the ruins of the brick kiln. The official word from Sheriff Mitchell Morgan (yes, Cecil Morgan's old man) was that Silas Tilley had prob'ly got to runnin' away from something, lost his footing, and fell down face-first into that brick pile a couple of times. That was good enough for most people, I s'pose, back in the day.

No one ever mourned Silas Tilley, really. Most people don't ever really remember him at all. I'm just tellin' you his story so you might know a little bit more about what makes that pus-jacketed flat-foot they call Cecil Morgan tick. I hope you can forgive me.

It's Just a Toe. It Ain't Proof

When I said that Daddy was a flagpole sitter, I s'pose most of you didn't really believe me. They ain't so many flagpole sitters nowadays—not the way they used to be. 'Course, I s'pose they ain't as many flagpoles as they used to be, neither. After the war people stopped puttin' up flagpoles the way they used to.

But Daddy, he would get out there and sit 'top them flagpoles like the best of 'em. He was once helpin' out and doin' a flagpole sit for that new department store over in Cotton City—a long, long time ago, as that store ain't there no more—and a man from some government agency asked Daddy to come and talk to him when he got down from that flagpole. Daddy warn't too much inna'rested in talking to no man from the government, but he said he would, and that was that. The man got on his way in a big, black government car and Daddy got back to his sittin'.

Well, Daddy stayed up on that flagpole for a few days, anyhow—I think it was through maybe a three-day weekend that the store had a grand opening or a big old sale or something. Sure, now I remember, it was a big sale. They had outerwear and toiletry items on sale 'cause of the tornado season coming, and Daddy was sittin' on a special made-up pole that they could make sway when they wanted to. They would pipe a sound effect over a phonograph and sway the pole and Daddy would let out a fake holler. People would gasp and one lady even fainted. When that happened, Daddy laughed so hard that he dropped the basket of fried chicken that Momma had sent up to him. Momma, you know, raised chickens for the State, and chicken was king at the dinner table in our house. Maybe it is in yours, too. That danged old fried chicken just came showerin' down on the people comin' outta the department store. Colonel Murphee got hit on the shoulder with a breast and it left a big ol' greasy spot on his fine white suit. He was mad, but he got over it.

On the day that Daddy came down, that man from the government was back, and I stood far away while he and Daddy talked. I saw him show some pictures to Daddy, Daddy shouted something at the man, jabbed his finger into the man's breastbone, spit on the ground and shoved past him. That man just got back in his big, black government car and drove off. Daddy walked back to where I was waiting and gave me a hint of a smile.

"Let's go, son," he said, "we got the whole world waitin' for us."

Sweet Apple Wood

(as told by Sonny)

"Sucker never could dance—he just hopped around until everyone was tired of seein' him sweat, and then he'd sing outta key and I'd be none too surprised if he pissed himself." Damon and Daryl would say things like that when they got to drinking, you know. They ain't never had no kinda gift for knowing the right things to say in strange situations, but it was just downright nasty to have them say things that were way out of line at those times, too.

Sure, you know it, you damned fool. But you know that they only said it to explain why that black-haired muffin designer from the big city always wore navy blue trousers. When someone urinates all over himself while wearing dark blue trousers, you can hardly tell. It is made especially difficult if the trousers are polyester, and you knew that was what every last pair of his trousers was made of. I only remember this seein' how I used to go into that insurance adjuster's office in Haverland and he had there next to his desk a little sign that said "Doing a good deed here is like wetting your pants in a dark suit—you get a warm feeling but nobody knows you've done it."

So I think I know what they were talkin' about. Funny how you learn things like that.

That raven-tressed sculptor of muffins would stand there at the urinal sometimes, so relaxed . . . so relaxed. He got to thinking that he was dreaming, and that the restroom he was in was just a figment of his dream—a dream that had him lyin' around in something soft and cloudy, like a pillow or something. He would be so relaxed, and the urine would flow, and then it seemed like something deep inside his brain would prod him with the question, "Am I thinking about dreaming while urinating, or am I urinating in a dream?" He would snap out of it with a start, and shake his head as though he were trying to make sure he was awake. Usually he'd pee over himself a little bit and have to wash more than he had planned on. Damned fool. That was just how he was.

And you knew it, and Damon and Daryl would say things like that when they got to drinking—they would laugh, and their big, saliva-covered lips would drip like a fat drop of honey runnin' off a chicken thigh or like something drippin' off some hog flesh, like some folk said lips can look. Hog flesh straight from the cuttin' floor. Straight from that cutting floor wet with the blood and all those strange kinds of fluids that spill out from a pig when you cut it right open and let the insides come right on out. My old neighbor (growing up) was a "belly grader," did I ever tell you that? Yeah, he worked at the hog plant and he graded bellies. Not nearly as bad as my friend Chris who worked there part-time and they gave him a small, sawn-off baseball bat to keep the hogs in line when they unloaded them from the trucks. Chris had to give 'em a good smack between the eyes to settle 'em down when they got all riled up. Damn. You can hardly do that very long and not develop some kind of problem. So shake those fatty lips, you fools.

The pieces of flesh looked a helluva lot like they came from hogs, in the way that hog flesh got that kinda almost human-ish kinda look about it, but when the police put that tape up we all knew better. The greasy, fatty lips cut from a face and left on the rim of that urinal were bad, but that bloody, sawn-off baseball bat on the urine-covered floor of the restroom was worse. A lot worse.

Guild to Host Hog Roast

by Respite Welk of the Crawford County Recorder

Local members of the Anglican Guild of Mary will host a hog roast this coming Saturday evening at the Switchback Estate on Rural Route 4 outside of Haverland. Admission is $6.00 for adults and $4.00 for seniors. Children under twelve and those suffering illnesses are invited to eat free of charge. The menu will consist of pulled pork, coleslaw, Elsa Mae Grabbethorn's potato salad, buttered rolls and cornbread, roast corn, gelatin salad, tangerine fluff, assorted pies and sweet tea or coffee. Milk will be available for seniors, children and the infirm.

The location of the hog roast was moved to the Switchback Estate after Crawford County Sheriff Cecil Morgan denied the guild's request to hold the roast at the pavilion on the square in Haverland. Sheriff Morgan stated the complaint of a local clergyman as the reason for the permit denial. "I don't wanna [expletive deleted] off any of the good Christian people of this county by panderin' to no secret societies," said Morgan in a prepared statement this morning. "We're decent folk here."

The dinner and festivities will begin at 4:00 p.m. on Saturday and continue until nightfall. Charlie Lincoln, local ward secretary, is sponsoring a clown from Cotton City to perform for the children, make balloon animals, and distribute free ice cream cups. Mrs. Lincoln will be offering free face painting for the children and youth.

The *Crawford County Recorder* has learned Mr. Peter Switchback has graciously donated all of the comestibles to be served that evening, and 100% of the monies raised at the event will be donated to an as-yet-unnamed charity in Crawford County.

Critique

(according to Ashley—you know,
from down at the filling station)

Work that smile of yours, Augustus Grayling. Work it as you work the crowd. Smile like a movie star and make your momma proud. She's never seen what you really do, so you can get away with it. Smile, you wastrel.

Crawford County was never big enough for you, and her people were never good enough for you. The sons and daughters of Crawford County always had stringy bits of fried chicken in their teeth and patchy grease stains on the fronts of their shirts—grease stains where the little bits of biscuit landed and rested undetected until well after lunch and then were brushed away absentmindedly while sipping our sweet tea and looking out over the corn and pea fields. This place was never big enough for you and they never did sell that "arugula" stuff down at Brompton's Market in Haverland. What the hell is "arugula," anyway? Sounds like a foreign-ass country somewhere.

We all know who you really are, Augustus Grayling, and we all know where you came from. And a lot of us know about the barn you nearly burnt down and tried to blame on the kids from Pole Creek. And I know all about the girl and the baby in Cotton City and one or two of us know about the boy and those filthy things in

Cotton City and it just makes us all sick. So don't think we don't know, Augustus Grayling. And don't you think that just because you use a fancy city name now that we don't know that your name is Augustus Grayling and it is always gonna be so. You are always gonna be that mean little kid from rural Crawford County who liked to say mean things to people just to watch 'em flinch. You ain't changed and neither has your life, really. You're famous now, but you were famous then.

People just couldn't stomach you, you mean little bastard. And we know that's true, as well.

Propaganda Due

The anger welled up in his eyes like the mercury in one of those old-fashioned thermometers.

"I'm gonna whup your ass!" Sid cried as he reared back his fist a second time and let fly with a vicious blow to the back of the boy's head. He heard a curious "pop." After that, he started punching harder and faster. He rolled the boy over onto his back and started directing punches to the boy's face, despite the helpless pleading and the screaming and the crying. With one massive blow he broke the left side of the boy's face and sent his eye flying loose from his head like a bobber on the end of a fishin' line.

Sid stopped throwing punches for a moment to consider what a strange thing it was to see an eye come loose from a person's head. He did not even take note that it was done by his own hand. With a chuckle from deep in his chest, Sid went back to his work.

After a minute or two of throwing punches, Sid noticed that the boy was not moving anymore, and the cries and the groans that had been coming out of the kid's mouth had stopped. Sid let go of the kid's shirtfront and let him drop onto the rocky ground. They were by the old brick kiln, Sid realized—a fact that had escaped him in his frenzied fit of violence. He looked at the bricks scattered around and reached down for a perfectly-formed paver. With a grunt he heaved it at the face of the boy, now lying motionless on the ground. The brick left a dusty, reddish mar on the kid's cheek. Sid retrieved the brick and repeated the process. Several times. Sid turned the kid's body over into a prone position and walked away.

"Switchbacks . . . they're prob'ly the ones who done it," he muttered to himself as he walked away, shaking and damp with sweat. "I know it had to be them, 'cause they done killed him with a brick. That's always the way they do it. My daddy said so."

Sid stumbled over the uneven terrain surrounding the brick kiln and he continued to curse as he made his way to a thicket of trees by the river. He dove in and began to rub himself vigorously—sending all the traces of blood out of his clothing, off his skin and right downstream. Having completed his ablutions, he walked upstream a few yards to a sunny clearing and dropped himself down on the riverbank. The sun filtered through the trees and danced on the water. In a minute, Sid was sleeping the contented, peaceful sleep of the innocent.

In his dream he saw a cornfield, ripe for the harvest. Walking in the middle of the field was a man in a grey flannel suit, unlike any man Sid had ever seen. The man didn't seem to be going anywhere in particular until he looked over and noticed Sid. Then the man turned to walk away from him, and Sid tried to call out.

"Hey mister," he tried to shout, but his lips could not form the words. As he tried to shout, he noticed his lungs not working so well, either, and he became aware of his inability to breathe. Somehow this was not distressing, and Sid just sat down in the middle of that big old cornfield and looked at the earth. Warm, soft earth. He ran his fingers through the soil and felt something under the ground. He scraped away an inch or two of earth to reveal a face, and as he looked at the face, the eyes opened and then the mouth opened and then the face began to sing. It was a song Sid had learned in Sunday school, but he could not remember the words. Only the melody was familiar.

A mosquito bite woke Sid from his peaceful slumber. Sid slapped the mosquito, leaving a bloody smear on his left forearm.

A strange kind of fear ran through his mind and he felt his bowels loosen and his trousers fill. "Damn, gotta wash off," he mumbled to himself through a nose full of tears and mucus. Back into the water he went, rubbing his forearm vigorously and grunting nervous sounds from between his teeth. He stripped his trousers and underwear off and let the crap float to the river's surface, where it was swept downstream by the current. He threw his stained white boxer shorts up into a tree branch, where they hung like a flag of truce. He relieved himself again, this time directly into the river. He remembered the school nurse saying that crap is supposed to float, so at least he figured he was healthy. "I ain't got malaria yet," he sighed.

Out of the water, Sid. Wring out your trousers. Find your shoes that you kicked off underwater. Get dressed. Stumble back to the clearing near the gravel road that heads back toward town. Laugh at your luck. Laugh at fate. Laugh at the kid lying face down on a brick pile. Curse the people responsible for it. Kid yourself.

Sid stumbled along the gravel road the few miles back to the filling station at the crossroads, where a lot of the group from the swimming hole had gathered and were drinking RC Colas. Damp, dirty and kind of shaky, Sid just gave nervous smiles to the faces looking at him. He told everyone that Silas Tilley had crapped himself and run home, as Sid told him he would whup his ass if he ever let that happen again.

Blink a few more times, Sid. Clear your throat. It had to be the Switchbacks who got to Silas, and he probably had it coming for being such an odd duck and for pinching your girlfriend's ass the way he did. Blink. Clear your throat. They're buying it.

They're buying it.

Sid looked absentmindedly at the fingertips of his right hand. The tiny whorls and ridges were clearly visible in the bright sunlight, and embedded deep in the little epidermal valleys was the dust and dirt and grime from a dark red paver. A paver that those same fingers had clutched with such passion, such strength. A paver that Sid had finally let drop one last time just before he walked away from poor Silas Tilley laying there on the brick pile.

A paver that would be with him forever.

Sid shook his head a few times and grinned. "C'mon, gimme one a those RC Colas, would you?"

Shame and Loathing

(as told by Jeb)

Tragedy serves me just fine, as it's only th' other side of comedy. Or is it victory? Whatever it's th' other side of, it serves me just fine, and if you wanna jes' sit right where you're at ('cause I know you're sittin' and you prob'ly don't wanna get up) then I can tell you a thing or two about the tragedy that made Crawford County the place it is. Only I ain't gonna tell you the whole story, as you prob'ly ain't got the time nor the stomach for the whole shootin' match.

Strange enough, it warn't no shootin' match that done it. It was more of a hog match. Well, a hog contest, really. And it ended up not bein' too much of a contest, neither. It was Jefferson Morgan, the grandfather of Sheriff Mitchell Morgan and yes, great-grandfather to Sheriff Cecil Morgan (or Sid as we like to call him but he don't like to be called hisself). That old dirt farmer Jefferson Morgan owned the grain mill outside of Pole Creek at the crossroads known as Blancher's. Well, sir, if you ever do go down to Blancher's, you're gonna see for yo'self a number of empty old buildin's from God-knows-when, as well as a couple of foundations that used to have somethin' on 'em. You also gonna see a single, solitary tombstone sittin' out there for God and the world to see.

It seems that a long time ago, just about the time of the War of Northern Aggression, Jefferson Morgan's father had jes' put the finishin' touches on his grain mill, and it was th' only one for miles around—th' only one in Crawford County, in fact. Well, after their army went through here, there warn't much left 'ceptin' Old Man Morgan's mill—the soldiers just marched on by without really much noticin' it, strange 'nuff. That left the Morgan family in pretty good stead, and 'bout th' only ones in the whole county with any hope of steady earnin's.

Well, long after Jefferson was born and got to his bidness of growin' up and learnin' how the world works and how it don't work, well he took over that mill upon his daddy's death. Seemed only right and made sense, too. And as it worked out, just after the war, the county got itself carved out of some o' this territory, and the little village that sprang up 'round the mill got to somehow bein' known as "Blancher's" and it got itself appointed as the county seat of "Crawford County," which no one actually pronounces that way 'ceptin' for travelers and salesmen. Jefferson Morgan was sittin' in high cotton and proud—like a coon suckin' on a catfish that got itself tossed up on the bank and forgot.

Th' only fly in the ointment was Jefferson Morgan havin' a likin' to gamblin'.

Seems old Jefferson got hisself in a bit of a wager with a man over in Cotton City over a hog-judgin' contest they was havin' over in Haverland. Jefferson put a load of money on a prize hog owned by Cyrus Tapper (yes, a grandfather or great-grandfather or something to Peasy Lou), and as it turned out, it was a lot more than money, in fact. In th' end, that hog ended up losin' the contest and Jefferson Morgan ended up losin' the mill. Morgan moved into a shack outside a' Pole Creek, and kept mostly to himself. Blancher's just started dyin' off 'cause the man from Cotton City just closed the mill in time as he had enough money and bidness of his own. Blancher's turned into the ghost town (or the ghost crossroads) that it is t'day, and Crawford County became the county without a seat—like a fat man without a chair.

Saddest part was that damned losin' hog. It wound up gettin' itself done in, apparently. One mornin' Cyrus Tapper walked out to the pen and seen it layin' there in the mud with its throat slit. Saddest thing. Cyrus done buried that hog just near the crossroads, and in time his son put that stone up over the grave, seein' how that boy loved the hog like a family pet and he was heartbroken over what happened.

No one ever pointed fingers or made any charges, but ever'one knew what happened. Seems ever'thing that Morgan family touches just turns to blood.

Piled High with Bile

(as stated by Cyril)

Never was a single one, no way. If'n I chose to go on up there to Cotton City that day I woulda thought to take along some cash with me, you know that. I ain't no sucker—'cause I didn't just fall off that melon truck, no matter what my daddy told you. He was drunk half th' time and he only took time to look at me if I was blockin' the path to th' outhouse. Bastard would haul off and cold cock me one—hell, I'd just drop to the ground like a sack'a bricks, even if he didn't really catch me a good one. I just dropped so th' hittin' would stop.

So, no, I didn't go up there that day, and I never did see no one runnin' back to Haverland. Didn't see a single person on that whole road, 'cause I was just workin' on my Ford just outside the edge'a town—damn thing started shootin' oil just while I was sprayin' that pea field—and I never did see no one. Not a single one.

If that bastard Cottreau says that I was up there then he's lyin' out his ass as well as through his teeth, 'cause he don't know what he's talkin' about. Dumb-ass pea-picker. I ain't been up to Cotton City in a whole long time. Last time I went was for that sale at the Co-op, when I got me some of that new stuff that s'posed to kill th' bugs but not dry your brain out except for maybe kids and little babies. But that's OK 'cause kids mostly don't like peas, no how. And, mostly, if you wash 'em good, you're OK.

So no, I didn't go up there that day, and I ain't seen no one runnin' on th' road back into Haverland, and I ain't seen no Sheriff Morgan, and I didn't hear no shootin'. I was just workin' on my Ford and sprayin' that field and I just wanna go home now. Kin I just get goin' now? You guys done with me?

Lost at the Fair

Little grease-mouthed Lucius DeWitt came runnin' at me one day when I was out plowin', and I ain't never gonna forget that day. Naw, it ain't 'cause of the plowin' and it ain't 'cause of the runnin' little grease-mouthed kid. It was 'cause of what went on in that one-room schoolhouse in Pole Creek.

"Miss So-and-So is daid!" cried that little grease-mouthed chimp of a white-trash pea-picker's son. "Miss So-and-So is daid! Shit-fer-daid!"

"You watch your mouth, you little crapper," I was forced to re-tort. I would have no such language used in my pea field.

"But she's daid! She dropped right there in the school house and she's daider than a rock. You gotta come. Summun's gotta come and help!" The little chimp was wigglin' and shakin' like he had a buzzin' cicada up his ass and I just wanted him to settle down and get the Hell outta my pea field, seein' as I had a lotta plowin' to do. But I got down and followed the kid across the field to the school-house. It warn't nothin' but a quarter mile jog to get there, but I was hot and sweaty when we reached the door.

Goin' in I saw all those kids just standin' 'round and lookin' at the floor like they was holdin' the biggest craps game in Crawford

County, 'cept for gamblin' bein' illegal. I figgered I knew what they was lookin' at and I was right. There was dead Miss So-and-So, just kinda sprawled out, a stick of chalk still clutched in her writin' hand, her glasses broken and lyin' next to her on the floor. It looked like she had kinda mashed that pretty lil' nose of hers on the way down—hittin' it on the desk or something. I bent down to investigate.

It looked like she might not be as dead as I or those dumb-ass kids in her class thought, 'cause I thought I see'd her breathin' a lil' bit. Her chest was movin' and I tried not to make it look like I was starin' at her chest in front of all the kids, but I kinda had to, so I sat there like a dumb-ass just starin' at her chest. I wasn't sure what to do next, so I yelled at one of the kids to go and run to the next farm over and call Sheriff Morgan.

After that I didn't know what else to do, but I had seen them do some artificial breathin' in a movie once, so I bent over and said "shoo" to them kids and then I put my lips on her lips and started blowin' like I was inflating that air mattress that I used to use when I was kicked out of the house that one time. I probably shouldn't have put my tongue in her mouth so much, 'cause it kinda hurt when she started coughin' and hackin' and came to and wrenched her mouth away.

"What the hell are you doing?" she cried, "What's going on?" She seemed kinda mad, but I figgered I was doin' her a favor by savin' her life and all.

"Yer gonna be just fine, Miss So-and-So," I said, "do you want I should keep goin' with helpin' you breathe?"

Well, suffice to say that after I got outta jail the next day I wasn't gonna go nowheres near that one-room schoolhouse. I took a little time off as I ain't never had a vacation, and I got down to the pond near Old Man Switchback's a few times and did some fishin'. The true corker was when I went to that covered-dish supper at the Methodist Church in Haverland.

I was standin' there, just breathin' in the fine, fine aroma of dear Mrs. Doulting's fried yam compote when I saw Miss So-and-So walk into the church hall carryin' a basket of what appeared to be cornbread. Now mind you, I wanted to get me some of that cornbread in the worst way, but I dare not be seen anywhere near her, what with the restraining order and all. Well, I just ducked under the nearest table and waited. I think it was Mr. Harper, the undertaker, that I was hiding under, 'cause I kept rubbin' his thigh with my elbow while I waited and I would hear him giggle and say, "Netty," which is Mrs. Harper's name. Anyhow, I just set a spell and figured I would quietly crawl out, get me some of that corn bread and high-tail it home when who should sit down at the table I was hidin' under but Miss So-and-So. This wasn't lookin' good, I guaran-damn-tee you, and it was only gettin' worse.

Miss So-and-So sat there and started eatin' her plateful of covered-dish morsels while I just sweated more and more, leavin' kind of a sweaty, oily patch on the tile floor of the church hall. Thank God they had big ol' tablecloths on the tables, so's it was harder to see if some big ol' dumbass like me was hidin' under your table. Only problem now was that I was sure I was startin' to kinda stink, 'cause I was sweatin' so hard and I've always had that glandular problem since I was just a little shaver. When I heard Miss So-and-So ask the others at the table if they smelled something like burning cheese, I know'd that I was making the stink like I sometimes do. My goose was likely to be cooked, but good.

It was then that I saw the trap door. It seems as though the Methodist Church hall had been built as something of a theater, as well, and they had some kind of a trap door goin' down to what was storage and maybe had been for an organ or an orchestra or some such thing. A trap door leading down to it was right underneath our table, almost directly under my sweaty old ass. Quick as I could I done opened it a crack, just big enough for me to slide through, and I felt around with my foot 'til I knew there was something beneath me. Down I slid until I touched the floor and I quietly closed that trap door above me.

I sat down there in the dark for a few hours 'til I heard what sounded like the last person leave the church hall. Just reversin' the whole process, I opened the trap door and crept back out of there. Out through the darkened church hall and out the door into the twilight streets of Haverland. There weren't no folks about, so I just quietly made my way back home and as I walked I thought about that danged Miss So-and-So and how much I wish that I never woulda' gotten mixed up in the whole thing that day in the one room schoolhouse in Pole Creek. And yet I couldn't help but think about really how nice it felt when I was tryin' to save her life. Maybe, like I said, I shouldn't have put my tongue in her mouth so much, but then I never knew 'cause no one ever told me how to save someone's life that way—I only seen it on TV and in the movies, and I just s'posed that when two people got their mouths together that way that it's how you're s'posed to do it.

Anyhow, I thought about this as I walked down that night through the couple of streets of Haverland. It didn't take all that long, seein' how Haverland only has about four or five streets and I ain't that good at thinking. We were a good match that way, Haverland and me.

Well, I never did quite get home that night. As I was walking back I got a little sick to my stomach and decided to sit down by the roadside and throw up a little bit if I needed to. As it turned out I didn't need to throw up quite as much as I thought I did, so I just sat there and I started thinkin' about how if that little grease-mouthed chimp of a white-trash pea-picker's son had never seen me that day in the field then I might not have had to sit all night in the dark basement of the hall at the Methodist Church. In fact, I was thinkin' that if I had that little grease-mouthed Lucius DeWitt there right then with me how I woulda whupped his ass no matter how young he is and how young I ain't. I just didn't care. I guess I was thinkin' that it was his fault that I did things The Sheriff and the judge said I shouldn't have done, and that I prob'ly got what I deserved, but I didn't think that this whole "restraining order" nonsense was a very good idea. I mean, what is a guy s'posed to do if he finds himself under a table with his elbow on the undertaker's thigh when that teacher with the pretty little nose walks in? What the Hell's he s'posed to do?

I guess I done fell asleep, 'cause I woke up under the bright Crawford County sun, realizing that it was Saturday morning and thank God I didn't hafta be at my chores 'til late in the day. When I sat up I saw two eyes lookin' at me from over a pretty little nose, and I realized it was Miss So-and-So. She was sittin' on a log just across from where I had fallen asleep, and as I looked around I realized that I had sat down and fallen asleep just on the edge of the yard outside of Widow Strathmore's big old house, where Miss So-and-So boarded. This all came to me in just an instant and I realized that I couldn't have picked a worse place to fall asleep even if I woulda been tryin' to do so. I got all scared and started breathin' heavy and I got to tryin' to scramble to my feet to get the Hell outta there when that pretty little school teacher actually up and spoke to me.

"Are you all right? Where are you going?" she asked with a voice that sounded like it might have been music. It was as pretty as her nose, no doubt.

"I . . . the judge . . . the restraining order . . . I gotta go," I replied, sweatin' like a whore in church.

"There is no restraining order," she said, smilin' with those perfect white teeth. "Mr. and Mrs. Harper told me all about what The Sheriff told you and they told me the truth about what you did, as well."

I was gettin' more than just a little woozy as she told me this, and I thought maybe that I had to throw up again like I felt last night, but I was OK.

"Thank you," she said, her straight white teeth smilin' at me still, "thank you for what you did."

That pretty little Miss So-and-So stood up, shook the dust from her sandals, brushed some little bits of milkweed she'd been playin' with off her dress and headed back toward the walk to Widow Strathmore's house. She got a little ways away from me and turned and asked me if I was gonn' be all right. I told her I was fine and that I 'precciated her bein' so understanding and all. When she was out of sight I got to my feet and staggered a few times—it seemin' like my legs didn't really wanna work none too well. I was OK, though, and I decided I would walk back into Haverland and use the toilet at the fillin' station, seein' as how it was closer goin' there than goin' home and I hadda go pretty bad. I walked along just kinda feelin' like you do when you're in grade school and Peter Switchback tells the truth to the teacher that you ain't the one who stuck the dead cat inna the basket in the cloak room and made it stink all to high Heaven. That's exactly how I felt and I was about as grateful to that undertaker doin' what he did the night before as I was to Peter Switchback when we were both in the second grade and he did that pretty good thing like that to me. It feels good and you just wanna breathe easy and have a slice of pie.

That's what I did. After I took a leak at the fillin' station I went to the diner and sat down for a nice slice of sweet potato pie. I was feelin' so good that I got to thinkin' that if that little grease-mouthed Lucius DeWitt came into the diner just then that I would buy him a piece of sweet potato pie as well.

He didn't come in, but that's OK. I still felt pretty good, and that pie was pretty fresh.

Advice and Sweet Tea

(advice from Aunt Elizabeth)

Remember, Peasy Lou, when you were a little girl how you used to say that standing and staring at that brackish pond water down by Old Man Switchback's used to make you feel all puny? Do you remember? I do believe it was nothing more than a mindset, my precious Peasy. For you were just a young lady and there was probably only one reason that the waters could have made you feel puny, but I was not one to share that with folks—least of all with the folks down at that greasy old ten-seat diner in Haverland. I knew that some would, though.

When you would stare and stare and stare and your eye would get caught up in a leaf or in a rock or in a bird sitting on a tree limb, it was then that you started feeling puny, wasn't it? I reckon it was also that very same time that you started feeling better and it was that very same time that you started feeling nothing at all. Peasy, your pretty gingham dress had such a stain on it, and I think that the few people who watched you walk back to Haverland had no idea what had happened, but they tried to create some stories in their minds. You know how those people in Haverland like to create stories in their minds, don't you, Peasy Lou darling?

I don't think that you ever said a word, but only got silent, and that is still the way you are today. Some will say to you, "Cat got your tongue?" but they don't know the whole story, of course. I would ask you if that bastard Cecil got your tongue, but I know he got something else and I wouldn't bring up his name to you, anyway. That name burns like an ember—a painful ember sitting deep in a lot of folks' flesh, because it was not only what he might have done to it and what, in a sense, he is still doing, but it is what he did to a lot of people and what he will never do for others. If ever there was a man who deserved a good swift kick in the man apples or an ice water enema or a rough pine stake driven through his godless, soulless, unfeeling bastard heart, I would have to say it would be that Cecil. And again, it would not be only for what he might have done to you, but for all that he has done and for all of that ancestral sin that the whole damned Morgan family has been soaking in for so many generations. From a bastard turncoat who went and might as well have fought with the invading army through the man who lost it all and tasted for blood that he might have revenge . . . and right up to Cecil himself—the ancestral sin of that family is like a black thread woven into an already filthy garment.

So I think that when you used to look at that brackish pond water and feel all puny, Peasy Lou, I think that there is just darkness in your heart that was planted there by a heart much darker. You ain't never been a bad girl, Peasy, and you know I love you like a daughter. You felt that way then, and I reckon you would feel that way now, no matter what people might say. I know what it is, and you know what it is, and lots of people *think* that they know what it is, but they have not the faintest clue as to the loom that wove that blackest, blackest thread—a thread that joined two garments and with time might be excised from the cleaner of the two, so as to make it that you don't feel so puny when you look at that brackish pond water down by Old Man Switchback's.

You're gonna be just fine, girl.

In the Emergency Room

with Lyle, back when

Yeah, I done tell'd you all 'bout how that damn fool got his arm caught up in the gears, but I was only wavin' at him 'cause it seemed like the right thing to do. I know'd that arm warn't ever gonna work again, so why shouldn't I try to make the best of what was goin' on?

Toddley just stuck it in there 'cause he was grabbin' for something that got caught on a little piece of wire. Maybe it was the piece of wire he was grabbin' for, but it don't really matter, do it? Anyhow, he just goes and grabs for it and when I sees it outta the corner of my eye, I turns and says, "You dumb-ass!" Then it sounded like when you break up a chicken for fryin', and Toddley starts screaming like you can't believe. But it warn't his fault—he was just grabbin' for something.

I don't think I coulda' really done much . . . that arm was floppin' ever which ways, and Toddley was already rollin' on the ground, gettin' dirt on the end of that fresh-bleedin' stump with the white tendon stickin' out. His shirt was pretty dirty too, so I felt kinda bad about that. He likes that shirt. He's probably gonna want more long-sleeved shirts now, seein how he won't want folks lookin' at his stump, even though they probably got it sewn up pretty good.

Toddley's gonna be OK, and I know he'll get back to workin' the pea fields, but he's probably gonna be a whole lot more careful now, that dumb-ass. He ain't gonna go grabbin' for things when they go in—it won't matter what it is that he sees goin' in, he ain't gonna grab for it. He's done learned. I know it. And I won't hafta shout at him when I seen it outta the corner of my eye, 'cause I ain't gonna see it no more. No sir.

You think we can go for lunch now?

Gerald's Pillow

"Ma'am, I will have to kindly ask you to please put some shoes on your feet." Mrs. Stella Jean Tapper (that would be Peasy Lou Tapper's grandmother; you know Peasy Lou, of course), was clearly annoyed at the slender young woman in the jeweled headdress and flowing robes who had just that very moment walked into her dry-goods store.

The young woman was definitely *not* from Crawford County—in fact, her type had *never* been seen before nor has it been seen since in these parts. I suppose there was the time that there did tour through our placid acres that vile and most wretched Mr. Havercroft, the ironmonger, but he was not the least bit captivating—only maddening. No, the slender, young, barefoot lady was in a league of her own, as it were.

Mrs. Tapper might not have forgiven nor forgotten the rather unexpectedly discalced maiden in her dry-goods store, but the entire county will perhaps never forget the wonderfully choreographed performance that she gave for a special public meeting of the ladies of the Eastern Star, wherein the maiden presented an interpretation of Egyptian mythology through the medium of dance and Miss Vidalia Sue Hornbeam (later Mrs. Vidalia Sue

Grabbethorn—you know, Elsa Mae Grabbethorn's mother) served the finest sweet tea and cornbread that had ever been offered at the Eastern Star. My, it was the evening, to be sure.

All The County look fondly on the sweetness of that memory—all The County and their pleasant, dying memory of so many years ago . . . save for the bitter acid in the mouth of Vidalia Sue. For while the barefoot maiden danced and stole the hearts of so many who watched with wonderment at the meeting of the Eastern Star, she also stole the heart of Gerald Pickering, to whom Vidalia Sue was betrothed. She danced into Crawford County, danced into his heart, and danced him away . . . back up north somewhere, some said to New Jersey. She was rebounding at the time from a failed marriage and had never been a bird to be tamed, anyway—least-ways by that starry-eyed son of a pea-picker, Gerald Pickering. He was never to return to Crawford County and within the season his broken life and his broken heart were washed up . . . washed up like broken bottles on the Jersey shore and Vidalia Sue (though crushed) went on with *her* life.

You would wonder if either Elsa Mae or Peasy Lou will be at the special presentation at the Eastern Star on the twenty-first of next month, wouldn't you? We will have to wait and see.

Jackpot

Never *once* did I care to know what that pea-picker's brother was thinking. I told you before all about that pea-picker and the things that *he* did, so I rightly do not have to digress and share any further thoughts about him, now, do I? Of course not, honey child. You just sit right there and sip that sweet tea that Mister Packy brought you. He did not bring you any sweet tea? Dreadful!

Mr. Packy! Please bring our guest a sweet tea . . . and be swift about it!

I do apologize.

Now then. Where was I? Oh yes, I was sharing thoughts about the pea-picker's brother. Well, I do guarantee that the day that the pea-picker was released from the county pen, his brother was bound and determined to fill his brother's cell, as it were. The only thing he wanted to do . . . the only thing he had any stomach for . . . damn, the only thing he had any *heart* for was seeing to committing a crime so as to keep up the family business and the name, you might say. So he went out and bought a length of chain and a shotgun that very day.

Sweet Heavens, but that pea-picker's brother had breath that smelled like fecal matter. It smelled so very much like a septic tank that no one ever felt fit to argue with him—they would take one whiff and let him have his way. So it was that he managed to borrow Old Man Donovan's pickup truck and cover with the story that he was going coon hunting in the dark and needed some way to carry a few friends. Dumber-than-dirt Donovan let him have it—partly because he believed the story and partly because he didn't want to stand face to face with that bowel stench.

The boy waited until nightfall and closing time for that gas station down at the crossroads. He pulled Old Man Donovan's truck right up to the place, put one well-placed shotgun blast through the glass doors, reached through and turned the lock. In he strolled, exhaling a great breath reeking of rectum.

The pea-picker's brother looped that length of chain right around the ATM that was inside, secured it, and then secured the other end to the hitch on Donovan's truck. He hopped back in and gunned that mother. That old ATM busted free of where it was, busted through the doors and came skittering right out next to a pump. That pea-picker's brother was just a-dreaming of all the meth he could buy with all the money in that ATM, and he knew with that much meth that he would find himself a little lady outside the Walmart. You know what I mean. He wasn't gonna be lonely, if you know what I mean and I certainly believe you do. Ladies love a man with that much meth, even if he has breath that reeks of a diseased colon.

Well, having freed the ATM from its moorings, the damned fool didn't know what to do, and when The Sheriff arrived he was still trying to wrestle the whole thing into the back of Donovan's pickup truck. Sheriff Morgan laughed so hard that he pissed himself and forgot to handcuff the poor bastard.

It was either the laughing or the pea-picker's brother's breath that made him forget. I am inclined to believe that it was his breath, honey child. I guess every cloud really does have a silver lining.

With the Ghost of a Switchback

Dial Reese Switchback died a tired, old man. There wasn't a soul in Crawford County who much disputed that, but then, it was back before the really big war and there were always plenty of men who were dying tired.

Old was up for grabs. That is, it was hard to say if Dial Reese was really all that old. Old was a different word a few generations back and Dial Reese was a different kind of man. Yeah, he was the flag-pole sitter and he was the grandfather to Peter Junior. Peter doesn't remember much about Dial Reese—only the stories that his father told him. Some things about Oreo cookies kept in a lard can. Kept there so long so as they picked up a slightly rancid smell and taste—so that when you were expecting the fresh creamy goodness you instead got something that reminded you of the grease dumpster out behind that Chinese restaurant in Cotton City. Yeah, that's the same one that Peter Junior used to go to for business lunches, but after several boxes of anti-diarrheal he switched to the Shoney's down the road.

So he was old and tired, suffice to say. Dial Reese had at one time thought about setting some money aside so that his wife, his two sons, and his baby daughter might have something to live on once his own days had run out, but he never really got around to that. Hell, he never really got around to a lot of the things that he thought he was going to do, and instead he would just spend whole days sitting up there on some stupid-ass flagpole.

The days it got windy were the worst. Dial Reese once got really sick while sitting up there and he had to drop a whole load of chunder down on the unsuspecting crowd below. People ran like you had floated an air biscuit in a crowded telephone booth. But hell, how many times have you ever seen a crowded telephone booth?

Well, enough about Dial Reese and his flagpole-sitting—it seems every damned story you hear about old Dial Reese has to do with his flagpole-sitting. I find it the biggest shame that no one ever really talks about his ghost, and no, I dont mean some kind of specter that floats around the Switchback estate and waits to scare the crap out of unsuspecting visitors. No chain-rattling, no late night moaning and no wine glass throwing, either. The ghost of Dial Reese Switchback takes his haunting seriously.

Ain't no place, and there ain't no time that is particularly beloved of this particular ghost. His is only a ghost for those who knew him well and for those who never knew him at all. I guess the ghost of Dial Reese Switchback is the ghost that we all could stand to have haunt our wheres-abouts, for it's a ghost that haunts when we most need it, but then probably when we least want it, as well.

Peter Junior sees that old ghost a lot, I reckon, and he knows exactly who that ghost is and why that ghost has to be hangin' around the way it does. When the light is low and his spirits are likewise, or when his spirits are in no particular place but he stands there, lookin' at a pea field, Peter Junior gets to hearin' that ghost talk to him. He will walk into the house and stare for a long time at that portrait of his grandfather taken in the Army camp before he went off to the war that they called the Great War. That portrait that the lawyer held for Peter Junior's father, along with a box of little nothings, while Peter senior was in the orphanage—that portrait is just about all that Peter Junior has from his granddad. A portrait, a spent casing from a French 75, and stories that his daddy told him about what a good man his granddaddy was. He never could help the fact that he ended up a flagpole sitter.

No one can ever help the fact that they end up a flagpole sitter. But I digress.

So the Switchback ghost roams the halls of Peter's heart, and tells Peter Junior what a good man he ought to be, and what a good man looks like and what promise there is in a life well lived. And Peter just takes it. 'Course, he wants to, and he's always been the kind of man that never needed to be told but always ended up doing the right thing anyway. Right Hell-on from the time he was just a little kid, Peter Junior just always seemed to know what was the right thing to do and the right way to go about doing it. And it was then, when he had done the right thing, maybe then it was that he saw the ghost. When he would look off into the distance and get that look in his eyes as though he was looking across a pea field or across the trenches in France or right across the very ocean into his very own heart, well, hell, that's where he was looking, and that's where that ghost was doing his best haunting.

So no chains would rattle and no wine glasses would go flying out of cupboards, but the ghost would walk and that ghost would get to doing his ghostly business.

That's what ghosts do, and when the ghost is the ghost of a tired old man you just expect a little less, I suppose.

The Devil's Apprentice

(as told by Jeb)

Collapsin' as he did with his trousers appearin' to be chock-full of something, we figgered ol' Sid was dead this time. Figgered he had died, and smelled like it too, and crapped his pants and now some unlucky apprentice undertaker in Cotton City would hafta be doin' a fine mess of cleanin'.

Sid always had a way of loadin' those trousers of his when the time was right and he needed to distract folks from something that just wasn't goin' quite right. I told you about this before, remember?

So Sid had just started his first day of takin' over from Old Man Morgan his pappy, bein' now like the danged third or fourth Morgan to wear that sheriff's badge in Crawford County, and Sid just never was too bright, tho' I wouldn't be the one to be caught sayin' things like that, so just you keep quiet, OK?

Well, Sid started the day OK but you can't keep a man like that too straight for too long, 'specially one who's got so damned much meat under his fingernails, like that oldish lady down the road used to say, "dat man, he gots meat unduh his finguhnails—he jes' gotsa be takin' dat meat home t' his old lady, so's she can saves it t' mix wit' de sawmill gravy fo' to go ovuh a mess o' bissits," and that Sid, he never had no need for makin' gravy, but he carried plenty of that meat home with him—it was the meat of other people's dreams and other people's hard work and other people's pride. Bastard. Wouldn't want to let that go to someone else, now, would you?

So Sid, when he did the worst as his way of startin' out, and he got drunk as he is likely to do and drove that big old cruiser straight on through a culvert and then through a fence and into a field where he cracked his damned big old head on the steerin' wheel and fell asleep while Colonel Murphee's two prize bulls wandered out of that field and onto the road, where the one with the biggest prize swingin' beef was summarily struck down by some poor kid from Cotton City driving a sweet 70-something Dodge Challenger (kind of like my brother had, all done up in pretty chocolate brown with that white vinyl roof), gunnin' it down the sad old highways of The County. Damned bull-meat all over the road, damned kid-meat all over the inside of the Challenger. Damned Cecil Morgan crapped himself like he always did and told a lie about his problem and he wound up givin' that poor damned kid a ticket when Doc MacFadden got finished puttin' the stitches in his face.

Sid learned how to do it, all right. He learned himself a whole lotta music on his daddy's knee, and he wanted to teach the whole damn world to sing his tune.

Interlude

I

There's ways of being, and ways of not being, and there's ways of having been. When we look back over all those yesterdays in Crawford County, we start to realize that there are a whole lot more yesterdays than we care to admit, standin' stark against the days yet to come. Who's in charge, anyway? We sure don't know.

I think sometimes there are things that happen in a place that stay there. I don't know if you know what I mean, and sometimes I don't either, as well, but I guess what I'm trying to say is something that my granddad tried to tell me once. We were walking past an old abandoned farmhouse in rural Crawford County, one where the shingles were just hangin' on for dear life and the windows were all put out either by blown debris or by thrown rocks. Granddad told me the story of how a family that used to live there had all been taken by the scarlet fever a whole long time ago, but how no one had ever forgot. He said that he thought it was a sad place, as they had all died, every last one of them to a soul, right there in the bedrooms of the house, the father going last and crying while he had the strength about his lost wife and lost children and even the strongest of them. It was only sad, not spooky or tragic, but none-theless, it was to Granddad as though the sadness never left the place, and for many years afterward—generations, even—it was still just sad. There was a lane that went past the house, a walking-type lane that folks would use on their walk home from church on Sunday, and it never mattered how spirited the conversations were that approached the place, they left quiet, subdued, and maybe even a little darker. Even folks who never heard the story (though I can't imagine many not having heard the story, frankly), even they said that they felt the same things in that place. Odd.

II

We already talked about what it's like when the night comes, but I ain't said a thing about what it's like when the rains show up. Most of the time, it seems, Crawford County is pretty dry. Well, yeah, I know I told you that Crawford County is a "dry" county, as you can't get a drink anywheres as it's against the law, but right beyond that, it is a *dry* county—we just don't get enough rain, it seems, ever, like we should. But when those rains do come, Lord, it is some-thing else.

If you ain't smelled Crawford County in a rain, you ain't lived. There is no finer place to be than on a hot dirt road as the rains start. There is first that smell—that fresh, distinctive smell of the rain coming—and it is followed by the smell of so many different plants that give off the most intoxicating smell when spotted with rain. And the earth. The earth.

The earth; the soil; that formerly dry, dry, dusty soil—the soil just drinks in that rain so quick it hardly even seems like the ground gets wet. I swear that sometimes you can hear that ground make a suckin' sound as the rain gets drawn deep down into the earth's belly.

I would be a whole lot happier about rain most days except for the fact that the rain, without a doubt, leaves a few muddy patches on the ground and I am ever so prone to find each and every one of them so that I go to trackin' that mud right in through the house. I seen muddy tracks be a source of rage, I mean to tell you. My Aunt Lydia, she had just cleaned the rugs one day when I was a kid, over playin' with my cousin Brian. She had just cleaned up and taken the better part of the day to do it. The rains came around noon and we stayed inside with the windows open enough to smell the whole thing but yet not get wet ('cause we weren't that dumb), and we were too engrossed watching the rain fall to see or hear that Uncle Walter had come home early from workin' in the pea fields. He made his way on in across Aunt Lydia's clean floors, tracking fresh mud all the way into the bathroom, all the way up the toilet where he was standing there and getting rid of a couple of cups of coffee. Aunt Lydia stormed in, madder'n a wet hen, and rushed right up to the bathroom where Uncle Walter stood relieving himself. She barged through the door, grabbing his belt and hauling him right downstairs and outside into the yard to the ancient outhouse all the while his jimmie flopping about from side to side. "Go and get *this* bathroom muddy, you two bit beet-weeder!" she cried, collapsing in a pile and a flood of tears. Uncle Walter was scared out of his mind and just zipped up his fly, shaking and sputtering. Aunt Lydia left the very next morning for a good long stay at that hospital out in the country near Cotton City.

More information than you probably need, but sometimes I just tell it like it happened. The stories I've been through sometimes make me think that no one could make stories up nearly as good as the real ones.

Damn.

So I guess that's about it for the rain. You get the idea. Rain's rain, I guess, except in places like Crawford County where maybe it's different.

III

I reckon you probably are all getting the idea that there's good folk in The County and there's not so good folk in The County. I hesitate to call 'em "bad folk," even if that is what they are. I guess it comes from my momma teaching me that we are all sinners even though we are made in the image and likeness of God Almighty. The guy named Kurt once used a phrase that went like *imago et similitudino Dei*. He said that was what that meant—the image and likeness of God. I said it sounded like a couple of those immigrant eye-talian baseball players who played for one of them big city teams with all the money. Like DiMaggio or Mantle. OK, so maybe DiMaggio ain't an eye-talian name, but I think Mantle is. You get where I'm going, anyway.

So there are those who are good and there are those are not quite as good as the good. But if I were really pressed on the matter, I would say there are actually a few who are downright evil. I wouldn't swear to it, and I probably wouldn't call them that face to face, but then, that is more my weakness than theirs.

When it comes to looking at good and evil face to face, there are some folk who look like they are so far to the one side that they wrap around to the other. I guess if you take some kind of evil dictator or someone for example—there's a really evil-to-the core kind of man, and he is so danged all to Hell evil and there he goes, running around getting people to either love him, look up to him, or at the very least follow what he says 'cause they're scared to death of the guy. He's gone and found himself so far to the evil side of things that the folk just love him and he appears like the most charismatic sort of folk you can imagine. Then there's on the other side of things, well, you just take Jesus, and there you got a guy who's so far to the good end of things that people just can't stand him no more. So what do they do with him? They kill him. It's just plumb crazy, that's all I can say.

Well that good and evil wrap-around thing happens not just in history but right here, too. Right here in Crawford County we seen it happen that way at times. I do believe you are getting the idea with how this all happens, so I don't have to go on and keep telling you about it. It's probably just better if you see it happen, anyway, rather than me tell you about it, because I think that the easiest way to see things unfold is to see them unfold. It is just a little bit like taking an adhesive bandage off a skinned knee. You'll see, if you don't already.

Partridge

I

Crescent coffee and crescent moon. There was always that Butter-Nut Coffee to drink in the old house. In the old house up on the hill where I used to be a child until I became a man. Butter-Nut Coffee and a piece of that cornbread that I used to love when I was a child until I became a man.

Becoming a man in time of hate and time of war except it wasn't a war and there was still only hate—hate that came out like a sort of slow-burning anger because there wasn't anything else to do in this God-forsaken place they called "rural" and I knew it. I kept coming back—I came back once and I knew I would always come back, even though there was nothing to do.

The heart of this place died. Died cold. Died old. Died young. Died, it did, but hell, I don't know that it ever had a heart that pumped and beat and lived. Hell, it coulda been just a lump of clay that laid there in the very chest of this place they called "rural" and never pumped or beat a lick. It just coulda laid there and looked like a heart when people stared at it, sayin', "That's a heart, 'cause I seen one and that's what they all look like."

Hell if it's a heart, hell if it ain't. Just settin' there like cold clay and settin' all lifeless. Go ahead, stick your finger into it and see if anything oozes out. You'll see.

My sister Bev stuck her finger into something once and she found out what it was. Worst part was that she held it up to her nose to take a sniff after she pulled it out and she wasn't too sure of what it was. She stuck it back in and lost the damned finger. People are always losing fingers when they stick them in places they don't belong. You notice that? Don't try it, but take my word for it—you go sticking your finger into something that your finger ain't supposed to go into and you gonna lose that finger, sure as hell. People stick other things where they ain't supposed to go and they get lost, too. The thing gets pulled off or it gets cut off or it gets torn out by the roots. There was the story of that man who had that happen to him. His wife did it, but I gotta leave that story for a time when we're back out by the barn, 'cause it ain't none too clean and there might be women and children who read this, so danged if I'm gonna tell you now.

But like I was sayin', crescent coffee and crescent moon. Crescent filth under a fingernail, too, I told you about that, right? Crescent filth and crescent moon. Crescent rolls if you're hungry, but more'n likely cornbread. Momma always made cornbread—she didn't care too much for crescent rolls. She'd make the kind from a tube.

When they took the tube out of Daddy's throat, we knew he was gonna die pretty soon, right then. He made that sound like he was gettin' ready to die. I know that sound is the sound you make when the end is coming and you can't hang in there too much longer. It makes kind of a rattly sound, like there's some loose slats in the chest—or like a man got louvers and the louvers are mostly closed but a few are broken or cracked and they're hanging in there all kind of loose and hanging in there just by a nail or two, and as the wind goes across them they kind of rattle and sound like that old house up on the rise outside of Pole Creek when a good west wind is blowin'. That's how it sounded when they took the tube outta Daddy's throat. I was gonna say something just then and there, but while I could think it I couldn't say it.

I was gasping through the tears. You ever done that? You get that pain that feels like you tried to swallow too much red meat without chewin' it proper, and it just sits there makin' a pressure on your heart. Well, I got to thinking that's your heart breaking and you just gotta sit there and take whatever is coming down the pike for you.

No good to be that way, ain't it? Yeah, I think so, and that's just what I said when they took the tube outta Daddy's throat.

So a crescent coffee and a crescent moon and a bloody crescent where that tube came out. And I cried like a baby—harder even than when my old hunting dog died. Them is the breaks, and there ain't no way of getting 'round it.

Crescent coffee, crescent moon.

II

There are connections and then there are connections. They ain't all the same, but I suppose you already know that.

Time there was that some folk didn't really care to be quite so connected to everything, but they wanted more to be connected to real live, honest-to-gosh real people. Seems these days, even in the small towns 'round here, that folks are more and more connected to stuff and less and less connected to each other. There you go. What are you going to do, anyway?

We all got connections but then there are days that we just don't want to be connected, the way that people are. Like the way I saw that one kid living or rather not really living but just barely existing in that hollow just south of Pole Creek. I told you about Pole Creek, I know I have. There was Appalachian dirt farmers came out this way long, long ago—same as there were everywhere in the whole danged county—and some of them settled in a little draw next to a creek down there a few miles away from Haverland (where most of the ones with good sense were settling and making something of a go of it) and sure enough when the first of them got there they got their way on up to a crossing by a dirt path that was coming through the woods, and standin' there, right smack dab in the middle of the creek was a long old pole, like someone had used it for pole-ing across the creek and made it and couldn't get the pole back outta the mud or silt bottom of that old creek. So the name done stuck. Pole Creek. There's been some from outside of these parts that asked me or asked others if it had something to do with people from Poland settling here and I never heard such a fool-ass thing in all my life. Ain't never been no one from Poland here, I don't think. Either they was too smart to make their way to Crawford County or they just wasn't bright enough. Who knows?

Anyhow. There was that kid that they found living out in Pole Creek, or rather in a spot out in a hollow just near Pole Creek. Well, it turned out his whole family had been living there for some generations, just barely making a life for themselves and raising a few hogs along with some peas and corn, and they all just lived out there in the hollow. The mom and the dad none too bright, but the kid was sharp enough to get to taking care of things when and if the mom and dad ever fell sick, which they did.

Yeah, the mom and the dad both come down with some kind of fever, some figured. The doctor in Haverland said the dad probably died first and the mom hung on a few days longer. Well the kid was not quite in his teens yet, but he saw to laying the parents out and burying them in the field out behind the house and then that kid took care of the few hogs that he had. It was only when someone for some reason went out there to try to sell something to the family or to ask them to pay up on some taxes or some such thing that they done realized that the kid was living out there by himself.

The kid was OK, but he was awfully quiet, they said, the rest of his days, and he used to like to set for hours and hours by himself and just stare away like he was watching something or someone walking across that old pea field and he would set there, then, and his heart they said had to be getting to being broken, 'cause that was the face he always wore and there was only a sad look in his eyes. Kinda sad and hungry, too, like there wasn't any kind of thing that he coulda eaten or drunk or breathed in through his very soul to make him feel full and warm and loved.

But there he was. So crescent coffee and crescent moon. Not knowing either one and I don't know them to this day.

No one seems to be connected today. They all think they are, but the folk in this county just don't have that kinda care that some ever had in this place. Who ever does? It all changes and so do all the folk.

Crescent coffee and crescent moon.

Poor Boy—Good 'Un

Caddick Black was not, as you might have imagined, an ordinary pea-picker. Caddick was in possession of a talent—some would call it a power—that made it unimaginable that he should spend all his days in a dusty field. You sit down right there for just a bit and I might be able to explain this to you.

We'll see.

Back before they put in that big old containment facility down near Blanchers, Caddick's family owned a few acres and they farmed a bit, sure, and they had themselves some hogs. Caddick's little sister was a skinny little thing that got kind of funny in the head and got to the point where she wouldn't eat almost nothing at all. For months, the better part of a year, I bet, she ate nothing but saltine crackers with cinnamon sugar on them. Oh, my, yes, it sounds kind of nice, I suppose, but there ain't much that a few saltines and some cinnamon sugar gonna do for a body, you know what I mean? Well, his sister just ate that and she kinda withered away, I guess you might say. In the end it was pneumonia that got her, but we all knew that the pneumonia only came about because of that constant diet not fit for a sparrow, let alone a young girl.

After they buried Caddick's sister, Mrs. Black (their momma), well she kind of got a little funny too. Some say it had to do with guilt and remorse over her daughter dyin' so young, and really that would be reason enough, don't you think? Sure you do. Well, after Mrs. Black got taken away to that place in Cotton City for a good long rest, Caddick was alone, seein' as how his daddy had drunk himself into the grave a few years prior. Caddick was maybe sixteen or seventeen or so, but he really had no abilities other than being able to just keep himself alive.

But like I said, he had a talent. Or some might call it a power.

When the autumn rains came and that Black homestead started getting a little leaky and the muddy rains started pushin' hard through the door and through the windows and right into Caddick's heart, well, he kind of went missin'. Some said that they saw lights go on in the house every now and again over that winter, and Dyke Cartwright said he saw a woman dash in and out of the house and speed away in a waiting automobile, but aside from that, no one saw that Caddick Black.

Dyke bought the fields the next summer, but not before a certain Candace Black, a dirty dancer from Cotton City, came to empty that house out and set a torch to it. That old clapboard shack just burned to the ground like it was a dry palm frond. Burned to the ground along with a lot of memories, I imagine. Candace, a tall, tall dancer with a low voice, strong hands, and a bobbing Adam's apple drove back to Cotton City and disappeared from the Crawford County radar screen forever. No one spoke about it much. No one really even raised an eyebrow, even if they were fairly certain what was goin' on.

I done heard that a couple years later the dancer named Candace got knifed by an angry man in Cotton City, after the angry man realized what was goin' on. So I guess there were some who raised eyebrows and some who had to speak about it. But it was always the wrong folks who were doing the raisin' and the speakin'. The wrong folk got to realizin' the truth, as well.

The wrong folk as far as Caddick was concerned, leastways.

O Blessed Iniquity

"I guess I couldn't care any less about you than I already do, and if you wanna know the truth I really don't give a lick about any of you Switchbacks." These were the mean, cussing words of a bastard of a Sheriff who didn't even need to cuss to make it sound like cussing, if you know what I mean. Those words came out so strong and so harsh and so full of the acid that percolated down deep in that void where used to be that man's soul that it just always felt like cussing when he spoke. My daddy used to say that Sid's daddy could turn anything into cussing and I guess it passed on from the father to the son. The father, it was said, could make people blush and turn away even if he were to read scripture. Not that Old Man Morgan would ever think to even pick up a Bible, let alone crack it open and even less begin to read. I could just imagine that if he did, though, it might be like the whole Heavens would open and angels would drop down to witness the event—or else the earth would split in two and demons would rise out of Hell. I would not be too sure which of the two would happen. Maybe both. Suffice to say we never had to find out because Old Man Morgan never opened a Bible, anyway.

So I was saying about Cecil Morgan, anyhow, that his voice was acid and his words were acid and the way he looked at you when he spoke was acid. And it was most acid of all, I remember, when he was talking to a Switchback. Switchbacks, far as I can tell, always end up standing for the right things, and there ain't nothing that Sid hates more than the right thing. You noticed that? If you haven't, you will at some point, I can tell you right now.

Well, those words that I told you, they were the words of a bastard Sheriff all right, but they were born a long time ago, I suppose. I last heard them when that damned Sheriff was watching young Peter Switchback set up a canopy tent for a hog roast to benefit the clinic in Haverland. Peter managed to get a lot of his business folk from Cotton City to drive all the way out and make big old donations for the clinic, and there were even those two who flew in from somewhere on the East Coast—two gentlemen that did a lot of back-slapping with Peter and laughing and talking with voices you don't ever hear around here. They were dressed real fine and had nicely trimmed hair—you know how you can sometimes see when someone is well-to-do and well-bred in how well they keep their hair trimmed? Well these two fellows matched Peter in that respect, seeing as how Peter always has nicely trimmed hair all the way around his ears and his neck is trimmed—none of that Neanderthal hair hanging off the back of his neck and there ain't no big old tufts of hair in his ears and between his eyebrows like some guys.

Anyhow, Peter got to hosting a right perfect party for the good of the clinic, and they managed to get the children's examination room added on just fine afterwards, but that bastard Sheriff didn't like it one bit and I think the pastor at his church wasn't none too happy either, seeing as how he had other ideas about how a whole lot of his flock should be spending their money rather than buying pulled pork to benefit a cause that old Peter Switchback done got himself behind. Rage was mostly what both that Sheriff and that pastor felt when they saw and heard folk praising Peter Switchback for getting a place built where little children could be cared for by Doc MacFadden and his colleagues.

Rage ain't nothing close to describing, though, what that bastard Sheriff felt whenever he looked at folk lookin' at him and knowing that they looked at others differently. The evil ones always want to be looked at as good and the good ones just don't care if they're gettin' looked at.

And I do believe it was likely that very day that the bastard Sheriff of a man—if a man is what you could ever call him—decided that he was not gonna let this upstart young well-meanin' man with the nicely trimmed hair and the clean neck get away with doin' something that others saw as good when all they ever saw The Sheriff doin' as being questionable. Bastards are bastards, strangely enough, and sometimes it don't matter what they're bein' a bastard about—you just know that they're out there gilding something for themselves or tryin' to spit in someone else's gravy.

Bastards always spit in other folks' gravy.

Like an Engine Block with Hair

"He done kicked Tiny!" Possey Pettigrew shouted at us all through the open door and the spit was nearly flying out his mouth and that uneven, kitchen-shear-chopped set of blond bangs of his flopped against his forehead as his too-big head bobbled around on his skinny shoulders. "He done kicked Tiny! Git! C'mon!"

Possey had a voice like someone had his swingin' beef in a stranglehold with pliers or maybe one of those grabbers that you use for pullin' cannin' jars outten the boilin' water. Could you see it? Steamin' hot cannin' jar grabbers right aroun' his swingin' beef? That's his voice, though, so's you get the idea.

Screaming and hollerin' in the yard by the barn meant that sure as hell there was something goin' on and it probably meant Tiny done got hisself kicked. Kicked hard and square in the man apples if I was gonna guess, 'cause it was a strained hollerin' and I was sure that I knew that feelin'. I had that happen that time we were all out workin' on puttin' in that fence on the back side of the land, and when I was bent over t'other way my cousin Teffer he picked up a rail from the pile that I was standin' near. Yeah, in fact I was standin' real too near that pile, 'cause when Teffer picked it up and gave it a little heft, well, the rail was between my legs and he snapped it right up there into my groin. Yep, just like you can imagine. Right in the man apples. Only I wasn't sure of how worse it would be from a horse.

Tiny was never too bright and he would do dumb things like spendin' his whole month of June's allowance on ice cream sandwiches from the fillin' station down by the crossroads and then getting sick and throwin' up that same whole month's worth of those ice cream sandwiches in the ditch out back of the fillin' station. Dumb kid. Dumb as the box of rocks like my brother used to say, 'cept dumb as the box of rocks that you threw out the window cause it was too dumb. I never knew what that meant, to be tellin' the truth.

So not-too-bright Tiny got hisself kicked square in the forehead by that shoed mule, and it left a little c-shaped crack that bled a whole lot and Tiny was even dumber than he ever had been and his sister Annabel had to watch out for him ever after that point. Well, after he got back from the hospital in Cotton City that is.

Tiny didn't go spending his whole month's allowance on ice cream sandwiches no more. He just sat around the parlor and watched the dust specks float around in the sunlight and maybe heard that shoutin' still in his memory if he got anymore memory left if that mule didn't kick it all outta his head.

"He done kicked Tiny! Git! C'mon!"

The Turn

So Tinny holler'd out, "Harper you asshole!" at me and started shakin' me, so as to get my attention, but I was too wrapped up in lookin' at the road in fronta me to really figure out what the Hell was goin' on. But I coulda told you alla 'bout how it done happened.

Me and Tinny was comin' back from Cotton City—yeah, we were just hangin' out, and we had only been drinkin' just a little bit—me more than Tinny, I s'pose. And I ain't real too sweet on him or nothin', so I think that I probably had just a little bit more than I shoulda, well, you know how it goes. I probably shouldn't have taken my shirt off, but we was laughin' and it was hot and the AC was busted in his old Ford, so I just took it off 'cause of that. It was stupid, I know, to go wavin' it out the window, so when I lost hold of it and Tinny hit the gas, I was like all, "Well, dang, what am I gonna do now," and I kept beggin' Tinny to turn around and go back and get my shirt, 'cause I didn't have anything else on under it. It was hot and all, you know.

So when that Sheriff pulled us over, I just felt all red and flushed, but what was I gonna do? When he came up to the car, I just sat there with my arms crossed over my chest, like nothin' was wrong. Dumb, I know, but then he done seen me of course, and me sittin' there with no shirt on, so he says like, "Miss, can you get outta the car," and he didn't even say please. Well, I did, and I thought he was gonna try to make me walk a line or somethin', but instead he just reached out and grabbed my chest with both of his rough, grimy hands and says I'm in deep trouble, how this is a felony and I'm gonna spend time in the county pen. I try slappin' his hands and pullin' away but he clamped down on my tits like he was hangin' on for life. I screamed at him and he hauled off and hit me one, and said I was gonna only make it worse by resistin' arrest and how that was gonna be another felony. I was scared crazy, I was.

He grabbed my wrists harder than I could imagine 'em bein' grabbed, and he hauled me back to his patrol car. I was screamin' for Tinny to do something, but he was just too scared to move. That Sheriff with the stinkin' breath threw me in the back seat and I just cowered up against the other side's door—I tried it but it was locked somehow and I couldn't open it. That was when I turned and saw that filthy sonofabitch start undoin' his belt and I felt like I was gonna get sick. I just screamed and looked for something to grab and hit with, but there warn't nothin' to grab hold of.

And it was then that I heard a pickup truck pull up behind the patrol car. I turned to look out the back window, and thank God I saw Mr. Switchback getting out his big old white pickup, and walking toward that filthy Sheriff who got back inna the driver's seat without even closing my door. As he hit the gas and the car started pullin' away, I piled outta that back seat and right down onto the gravel on the side of the road without even thinking. That Mr. Switchback bent down to see if I was OK and when I said I was fine, he sprinted back to his truck, got in, and started chasing after that damn Sheriff.

Craziest damned thing you ever did see—that white pickup chasin' after The Sheriff's patrol car that was racin' to get away like a bat outta Hell.

Gutpile

(as told by Uncle Shiloh)

Praisin' the day a'fore your head hits the pillow is jes' plain dumb, and I don't care what your feelin's is like when I says it.

It wasn't no special day no how. It was raining, and Cliver Bennet, that crazy farmer with the black, hairy tongue (I ain't makin' that up, neither), he was sayin' that 'cause a how it was sunny out with no trace of clouds in that perfect sky, well, he got to sayin' that the devil was beatin' his wife—so it was ever' time that it was rainin' under a clear blue sky where the sun is shinin' like it never shone before.

Devil was beatin' his wife.

So you always got to praisin' the day so early on and the day could get goin' right or the day could take a turn for the worse and when it done that, well, there ain't no tellin' how bad it might get to bein' by the end. Beginnings is beginnings and ends is ends, but summer's about in the middle and you always gotta know that there's a point where it could go either way. I reckon you know what I'm talking about, don't you?

Eustace! Call that dog o' yours away from them chickens out here! He gonna get to 'em if you ain't careful! Git, you damn dog, you! Now git!

So if I told you a thing or two about that Cliver, I bet you would go on and tell half the county, now, wouldn't you? Dang. It don't matter no how.

Cliver got that black, hairy tongue, and that ain't no lie. He ain't had it all his life, but long enough so that no one really much remembers him without that kinda tongue. I reckon that when you got a black and hairy tongue it probably seems like you had it a lot longer than you actually do. Some says he got it on account of all the coffee and tea that man drank, others said it was on account of the tobacco he smoked, which was like a chimbley and all the time, no foolin'. He played the fiddle some, pretty good too, and when he played he opened his mouth and closed his eyes, so ever'one could see his hairy black tongue, but with his eyes closed he could never tell that the whole room was lookin' at him and at his black and hairy tongue.

Eusty, dammit! Git this dog! I'm gonna whup his ass outta here if you don't come and get 'im!

Damn. Now where was I? Yeah. Well, it was black as the ace of spades and hairier'n an ape, and all the world would see it when he played at the barbecue and sat there all mouth agape, hairy tongue stickin' out jes' a little bit. And it was at a barbecue just like that, where he was playin' with his eyes closed that he seen the prettiest woman he ever did lay eyes upon. It was after he opened his eyes, of course—not whilst he was still playin' with his eyes all shut, mind you.

He stopped after a good try at Orange Blossom Special and opened those hazel eyes of his that were more than just a little crusty and he seen a vision so pure, so fair, so remarkably like his own mother that he nearly passed right out. She was visiting from Cotton City and no one knew her name. Visiting friends in Haverland, more'n likely, but no one ever owned up to it so no one ever did much go askin' around—though it wouldn't a done no good even if they knew her name and shoe size.

Story goes that Cliver then got some mickey built up to go talk to her, and when they get to exchangin' pleasantries he opens his mouth to speak and make a little laugh like he was prone to do—a flat-tongued laugh that came out, "Hah!" and caused him to splay his black hairy tongue 'most flat and open to the world.

People see things when they's already sensitive to certain such things, and Cliver done seen that girl from Cotton City flinch and make a small face when she seen his tongue. It looked like she had made the kind of face you might when you drink a grub in a glass of cider and only realize it when it's part way down your gullet. She seen the tongue and he seen the look, and he never did see her again.

That afternoon old Cliver put down the fiddle and picked up the bottle. I think it almost had to be a couple of bottles, really, and he hit 'em hard, I mean to tell you. Hours went by and Cliver slipped away, headin' out back from where ever'one was for the barbecue.

When Peter Switchback found him, though, he was passed out in the lavatory of the Buckleman farm house, bloodier'n a stuck pig, havin' made the biggest mess on the white tile and linen. White-washed wainscoting was never gonna be the same and Mrs. Buckleman ended up wallpaperin' and paintin' that next fall.

Anyhow.

Yeah, he had got hisself good and drunk on corn whiskey and got a hold of old man Buckleman's straight razor. He put that old cutthroat to his tongue, back and forth, without benefit of strop or soap, and he hacked that black hair right off, makin' his tongue look like someone had gutted a deer in his mouth. He didn't feel no pain, I guess, or the shame kinda' numbed it. One or the other.

Cliver's dad had fought the Germans and his granddad fought the Germans, and that granddad's granddad fought the Yankees, but Cliver jes' fought himself. Hell, he nearly got bloodier than all the others put together, but that tongue came back hairier than ever and lookin' for all the world like a pile of God-knows-what—lookin' jes' like absolute scarred-up, black, hairy hell. Sometimes things don't work out the way you'd hoped 'em to, 'specially when you had too much corn whiskey. So like Cliver would say (before he cut up his tongue), you can't praise the day until your head is on the pillow and even then it might not be too wise.

Eusty! Git that dog o' yours! Git! Damn dog! Now git!

If Pressed

Cal was always a miscreant, though I never really was sure what that word meant, anyway. I think I would say he was a trouble-maker, and be done with it, 'cause Cal never knew how to treat a lady, and Cal never knew how to treat anyone for that matter. He was just a troublemaker.

We went out to that old quarry one summer afternoon when we were just kids and Cal insisted on bringing a bottle of cheap-ass whiskey along with that none-too-bright kid from the neighbor-hood named Kevin. You remember him, I know you do. He had that bowl haircut and a nose that went in two different directions at once. I hated that nose, and Cal did too, I think, but Kevin was fun-ny as hell, seein' as he could do imitations of all our favorite arcade games. He could make all the beeps and sounds from all the best ones. Pac-Man, Zaxxon, Ms. Pac-Man, Donkey Kong. All the good ones. He would sit there like a damned idiot and make all those beeps and whistles and little bitty songs that went with the games. It cracked us up, 'cause Kevin didn't know we were laughing *at* him. He just thought we were laughing *with* him. Damned idiot.

So we got out there to the quarry and Cal opened that bottle of whiskey with a crazy look in his eyes. He pulled long and hard on that bottle and then passed it to me. I tried to suck a long old drink out of it, but the smell got to me and I kind of gagged. Kevin made that "doodley-oot dee doodle-oo" sound from the Pac-Man game, Cal laughed, and I blew whiskey outta my nose. It hurt and burned like hell, but it only made Cal laugh harder. Kevin didn't even know what was goin' on and he thought Cal was laughin' at *him*. This made Kevin get louder than he already was, "DOODLEY-OOT DEE DOODLE-OO," and so on.

I sat there just trying to catch my breath from the whiskey goin' outta my nose, and Cal just laughed and took another pull from the bottle. Dumb-ass Kevin got up and started lookin' around the edge of the quarry, diggin' through some scrubby little bushes that were growin' there. I wiped my nose on my shirtsleeve and noticed a little smear of blood mixed in with the whiskey and snot. I didn't really pay it no mind, seein' as how I had blown that whiskey out pretty hard.

I was just fishin' around in my pocket for a hanky when Kevin starts screamin' his ass off and hoppin' around like he had a leech on his willy. Cal ran over to where he was by the bushes and just said, "Damn." I forgot about findin' the hanky when I saw the look on Cal's face, and I ran over to where the two of them were.

It was an arm all right, with a part of a nice shirt still on it—starched cuff and all, too. There was even one of those college rings on the ring finger. There really wasn't any blood to speak of, strangely, but we could see where the meat and the bone was stickin' out—it looked like when Uncle Steve shot that deer and cut it up himself so as to save money. I went over to his basement when he was cuttin' it, and I saw it layin' there . . . and this arm with its meat and bone looked a lot like parts of that deer.

Well, we sure as hell didn't know what to do, and dumb-ass Kevin was freakin' out, so Cal said he thought I should carry the arm into town while he blindfolded Kevin and led him back home by a rope. I thought this seemed pretty good, but the arm felt kind of funny and soft when I picked it up.

"Can't we just throw it into the quarry?" I wanted to know and kept askin'. Cal said we couldn't and that I shouldn't be a dumb-ass, as that was Kevin's job. I just shut up and carried the arm.

We gave that nice, respectable-lookin' arm to Sheriff Morgan, and he thanked us. He never said anything about us smellin' like cheap whiskey and me havin' it all down the front of my shirt. I figured he was too interested in the arm to really care about how we smelled. The arm had kind of a different smell to it anyway, so who knows?

That was more than twenty-five years ago, and we still never did hear whose arm it was. Dumb-ass Kevin got hisself hit by a train a few years back, and Cal is in the county pen, so I told him that if I ever did hear any news about the arm, I would come and tell him or at least write him a letter.

And me? Well, I just keep workin' my job at the hog plant. I make pretty good money and it gives me a lot of time to think—to think about things I want to think about. Like that arm. And about the sounds that those old arcade games used to make.

This? Naw, I ain't been to college. I don't know if I'm s'posed to wear it, but it sure looks good, don't it?

Deuteronomy

I

Headlong he fell . . . headlong down the embankment into an over-grown drainage ditch. Peter and all of his 175 pounds of Switch-back frame fell headlong while a pus-jacketed skin-eater looked on with a corn-eating grin.

"He ain't gettin' out," Sheriff Cecil Morgan said to the dough-faced deputy standing nearby. Dough-faced in visage, not in politics; dough-faced in heart, not in mind. "He ain't gettin' out. He ain't wakin' up."

Two previous Sheriffs Morgan had owned and carried the small, wooden-handled revolver that Cecil carried in his sweaty right palm, and with it each of them had erred and strayed and sinned mightily; erring and straying and sinning was nothing new to the revolver, and certainly not to the pus-jacketed skin-eater that held it now and looked down into a drainage ditch at an unconscious Switchback—a position the two previous Sheriffs Morgan would have envied and coveted.

Some there are who do not savor the sweet taste of irony; many there are who do not choke on justice, and yet some are so small in the mind to miss it all. You're familiar with folk like that, ain't you? 'Course you are.

Something dark happened there in that ditch, and something light had happened just a bit prior. And while one man thought he had everything restored even though it was a small thing, another man lost what he thought was but a small thing even though the man who took it thought it was everything. And there was just a little bit of irony and certainly not the least trace of justice. But the man who knew it was a small thing could not have cared the least for justice come by man. Man can only do so much, you know. He knew it too. Only that pus-jacketed skin-eater thought that man could do it all and that man could take it all away.

Damned stupid pus-jacketed skin-eater. He ain't never gonna learn, I do reckon.

II

Death is funny, you know. Well, it really isn't so funny as it is *odd*. That is what I have always maintained, leastways. And the fact that it is odd gives, it seems, certain people rights to talk about it different than some other people might. Well, I mean like that under-taker—he seemed to have this way of talking about it that made you wonder if he wasn't some kind of seer or some kind of prophet, 'cause, damn, he sure didn't seem scared in the least and he sure seemed to have some kind of prophetic knowledge about death. Crazy how that is, isn't it?

Men sometimes don't really know how it is when things are prophetic, do they? No, I reckon they just don't. And when that prophesyin' is about things like death, well, I s'pose that most men just want to turn away and look at something nice for a while. Don't we all just want to look at nice things from time to time? Yeah, I reckon we do.

But death don't ever look all that nice. There are the times when death has been a long time coming and the body who is meetin' up with death probably just needs to get on with it—there are *those* times when death ain't as bad as it is at other times. Still, there are those other times, when the death just don't seem to make a whole lot of sense . . . when the person dyin' is a young child or a person in the prime of life or a person with a whole lot of things to do yet, well, it is those times that there don't seem to be a whole lot of sense, and yet death comes just the same.

Humble Access

(as told by Jeb)

Patience don't know what Patience can't see. Patience had to spend near almost every minute of the day closed up in her room, didn't she? Yessir, now, she did. Patience tried to ruin that poor Switchback boy and the whole county knew it, but the whole county knew, oddly enough, how good that Switchback boy was. And is. And probably always going to be.

They was in high school, if I recall. Peter was a strapping lad and involved in his church—only a handful of boys were, if I remember correctly. Very unpopular boys. Peter spent a lot of his time organizing things. Food drives, nursing home visits in Cotton City, that sort of thing. He really had no time for messing around and that was what got Patience's goat, I believe.

That Switchback boy had turned down her advances a number of times, for she was a dark child, something not right and something not altogether clean about her. She wore clothing that was just on the verge of revealing too much and she wore makeup to school. Some said that she had a tattoo that she had placed somewhere that the discreet eye would not see—a tattoo she got on a trip to Cotton City—a trip taken with an older man who drove a fast car and liked to drink whiskey. Patience had more than whiskey and tattoos that she was keeping a secret, I can only imagine.

She wanted Peter Switchback. She wanted to possess that boy and she had nothing but carnal desire for him. A girl of seventeen. Such tragedy. Such shame. She chased him, in a manner of speaking, for months, and the whole thing came to a head and popped like a ripe pimple on an afternoon in early spring. Popped just like a ripe pimple when that girl came cryin' and huffin' and puffin' and walkin' out of the annex of the public school after hours on a half-day of school, walking into the teachers' meeting room, walking in half-barefoot and a torn dress revealing her left breast, a scrape on her one knee and crying out to the half-dozen educators present and claiming that Peter Switchback had got a hold of her and done unspeakable things to her and he was a monster and that someone should call Sheriff Morgan and how it was that she was so forsaken as to now be defiled and that Peter Switchback must suffer and pay for this. For she had seen Peter alone in the library and knew he would not have an alibi and would be unable to answer her charges.

Poor Patience. But Patience don't know what Patience can't see, and it was poor Patience who had torn her own dress and scraped her own knee and kicked off one shoe and raised her own ruckus in order to vilify that fine young man who was on that very afternoon actually taking a timed exam for some national academic merit society. As truth bore out, Peter had completed the exam in record time with a near-perfect score and immediately gone out for a peach phosphate with Mr. Withers, the biology teacher and track coach. Peter was blissfully unaware of the things being said about him while he and Mr. Withers discussed his chances for a bright future at a state university.

I saw Patience just the other day, working at the discount store in Cotton City. I believe she is with child again, although she still ain't married as far as I know and as far as folk tell me. I couldn't bring myself to ask her face to face, as I just don't know her that well. Some folk turn down every chance for good to do that which is most likely to bring them pain, while others just seek out pain to avoid doing good. But you know what they say. Patience don't know what Patience can't see.

Better Sense

(as told by Marcia)

Leavin' as I was, I saw that I had better get some food put together 'fore I left. I was gonna be goin' away from Crawford County for the first time ever, and I didn't think I'd ever be comin' back. I done been wooed by a crystal vendor on the West Coast—a man I done met through an ad in one of them magazines—and I was gonna go out and marry him. It all seemed a little odd, I know, but I loved the idea of bein' a mommy to a couple of Chihuahuas.

I never even knew, really, that there was much out in the world aside from these pea fields and the cotton. I been up to Cotton City once with my aunt Della, but that was just for an afternoon. We had phosphates or sodas or something she called 'em. It was next to an ad for some kind of soda phosphate or something like that where I done seen the advertisement for meeting your dream and I done bit like a catfish on a tickler's thumb. Little did I know that there was a strange chapter awaitin'.

As time wore on and I was s'posed to head out west, I got a letter from the orphan who used to live near Blancher's but had moved up in the world and was doin' OK. Peter Switchback it was, but it was not so much a letter as it was a clipping. A newspaper clipping about the fella I was goin' to marry. Peter Switchback ain't never been someone to hurt another person, let alone speak bad of another human being. Like my daddy had said about him, Peter Switchback is so clean he wouldn't say "crap" if'n he had a mouth full of it. That's pretty clean in my book.

Anyway, Peter sent me a clipping of the crystal vendor and how he was running a charade and the whole of his supposed crystal therapy clinic was nothin' more than a front for a puppy mill. That's right. A puppy mill. He was raisin' little baby Chihuahuas and sellin' 'em for profit. The mommy Chihuahuas had their teeth all taken out so's they wouldn't fight with each other—you done heard of this, I know you have. I read it somewhere. Well, Peter found out about it and just dropped a friendly clipping in an envelope through my screen door just a couple of days 'afore I was gonna get goin'. I saw the envelope when I was packin' some potted meat and stuff for makin' frybread—I didn't know if they had potted meat on the West Coast. I read the clipping and I felt like all the blood drained outta my face and I just hadda sit down.

I hate people who run puppy mills. Don't you? I hate it when people hafta have those damn purebred dogs. My black dog is damn good, pardon my French, and he is the best dog you can imagine. What with all the strays and shelter dogs out there I don't see why anyone has to have a purebred. 'Specially not from a puppy mill.

I had all that money spent on a plane ticket, and I lost it all, but about a month later I got another envelope with the full amount of the plane fare in it. It was anonymous, but I done learned through the grapevine that men from Peter Switchback's church done raised the money over coffee one mornin'. I hear they're always doing things like that for people and charities and such. They think no one knows who it is, but this is a small town.

But I know Pastor Williams says the Switchbacks are bad folk, though, even though they helped me out of a tight pinch and I guess they got a soft spot for puppies and old folk and the poor and the hungry. Least some do, anyway. And some know how to do the right thing, as some do anywhere, but I want to shout it from the rooftops about the dogs and the dark that is in some people's hearts—the some who lie and the some who got greed comin' out their pores.

I was glad I had the potted meat on hand, anyway. My black dog, Barker, he and I sat down on the porch and shared that can of potted meat and I said a prayer of thanksgiving for Peter Switchback and those friends of his.

Harper, Better than Late

Standin' at that Switchback boy's grave was the hardest part, I really thought. There wasn't really anything he was gonna do to cheat the Grim Reaper that day, I suppose, and I know that, but knowin' why he died and who he done died for makes it all that harder to swallow. Kinda like dry beefsteak when you ain't got no glass of water to wash it down and that big old bolus of chewed-up meat just hangs in your gullet like a wad of patchin' plaster. One of the Tapper children died by chokin' on something, and I think it might very well have been dry beefsteak, for I know that meat can be especially hard on a young 'un that way, mostly in terms of hot dogs and other such sausages—as it is said they so nearly approximate the diameter of a little child's windpipe.

And that is just how I felt, standin' at that Switchback boy's grave.

Yet I should hardly call him a boy, for he was well into his fourth decade of livin' and he would have made it a lot further had he not been so morally grounded. I don't know that "grounded" is the word that I need use, but it serves as well as any. Mr. Peter Switchback (the young Switchback boy) always believed, he said, in the brotherhood of man and the fatherhood of God. I s'pose this colored just about ever'thing he ever done and ever'thing he ever hoped to do. He done learned this from his poppa, who done learned it from *his* poppa, far as I can tell.

That boy went outta his way for that louse of a man, that Cecil Morgan, he went outta his way to keep him as he thought he had to be. Cecil thought one thing, Peter thought another, and ain't that just like how it is? One man thinks one thing, one man thinks another. And if chewed-up meat can be hard on a young 'un, well, I just know that the differences between men can be even harder—and not on the young 'uns, mind you, the differences are hardest on grown men; grown men who take it all to heart and that good man takes bad things to heart and sees iniquity and the bad man takes good things to heart and sees foolishness and that's just the way the whole matter lines up. So while Peter Switchback saw in Cecil Morgan someone to be saved and aided as he might have been failing as a sheriff, well, old Cecil Morgan just saw Peter Switchback's goodness as a mere folly—a folly that made no sense in the world old Cecil Morgan lived in and the world he wished so desperately to control. He done seen it as something more than folly, too—he saw it as something to be gained; something to profit from. He saw each and every thing in terms of what he was gonna get out of it—was it gonna help him? Was it gonna make him rich? Was it gonna get him laid? Was it gonna keep him in office for another term? If it didn't or couldn't or wouldn't answer yes, well he had nothing to do with it. It was all about coming out "smellin' like a rose," as my daddy used to say. Daddy also used to say that if you wanted to hit a man hardest then you had to hit him in the wallet—that didn't mean punchin' him in no ass-cheek, neither. Daddy also said that if you needed an answer to what drove most men, then you had to "follow the money." Daddy was pretty much accurate in things that he said, you see, and this all applied to the damned Cecil Morgan more than to 'most everyone I knew. Follow the money.

From Beyond the Grave

The sourwood is forever green and that is not to say that it is an "evergreen." I suppose you know what I mean by this. I have always understood "evergreens" to be pines and spruces and hemlocks and firs and such. Whether or not the sourwood falls into one of those families, I have no idea. I don't think it does. Whatever the case, I see now that it is always green. My brother spoke of this, and a man once told me this, but until I saw it with my own eyes I had no idea that it was true.

The sourwood upon which I rested my weary gaze was small and light, and it had been laid there by a very well-meaning friend. But this man was more than a friend, and I knew that. The sourwood, therefore, took on added significance, as it was something of a gift or a token. Yes, a token. That is the best way to describe it—a token.

When at first everything changed, I was a little surprised, but now I suppose I am getting used to the idea. The sun at midday is warm, but when we are called from labor to rest there is a warmth much, much more pervasive. That sort of warmth pervades and persists, and we look to that warmth as the only sort that might last a little while longer.

When the hour of rest has ended, I know that we will be called back to labor, but I am certain the ones who go on to labor will be quite serious about what we are doing, and there will be a great sense of joy at being called. Haven't you just felt that way about your own work from time to time? I am certain that you must have felt that way—I know that I have, and I am no exceptional individual.

I think back over the years and reflect upon all of the good men I have known, and what hard workers they all were. Maybe that is the measure of a good man, for some, but I suppose it still goes even deeper than that. I guess it goes all the way to that white-hot core of the man that burns—fueled with his passions. Some men have passions that are a little less useful than others. They have passions that read like the litany of passions you might expect. Sex. Money. Fame. Power. Yes sir, I have known some men like that, and I suppose we all have known a few like that. God willing, some of those men find their passions change over the years, and they might adopt or develop different passions. The passions that really get you the farthest down the road are those which are a bit less glamorous, I suppose. Some men have a passion to create, some have a passion to compete, some have a passion to wonder and experiment and explore. Some men just have a passion for doing good and for making things a little better than the way they found them. I like that sort of man. I have always liked that sort of man. I suppose that if you asked most folks, they would agree, for that sort of man is welcome in any place.

Well, I was going to get to talking about the hour of rest, but perhaps that is not necessary, aside from saying that if you who are still at labor believe that you are eager to be at rest, well, I do believe it is even more the case that those of us at rest are all the more eager to return to labor. This may just be a case of the grass always being greener on the other side of the fence, but if one is perceptive, one will even notice that (even in the midst of labor) the fruits of labor are more to be savored than the fruits of our rest. Toil, and the whole world benefits; sleep and you reap alone.

◆ ◆ ◆

Virtue is a curious thing. Virtue is not something that you can suddenly just choose to have, and virtue is not just a thing that someone can force a man to exercise, of course. Virtue is that to which a man agrees with every fiber of his being. It cannot be taught, but it can be learned. And then again, I knew one man who always said that it can be taught but it can never be learned, for it must be developed, the way that the taste for blue cheese or the taste for good, good whiskey cannot be learned but only developed over time. And developed, mind you, that it does not become a passion in the meantime. You thought I had forgotten about that? Heavens no, my friend. It is all a matter of balance and a matter of moderation, for even the man who embraces very good things can go right overboard and find himself sinking down into the depths of a passion that has got him held fast.

Be careful that doesn't happen to you, all right?

So virtue, then, grows. Sometimes it comes in fits and starts and other times you don't even see it coming. It just shows up over a whole stretch of years and when you don't even realize it, well, there's virtue, sitting right there and coming out when a man needs to exercise it. Thanks be to God for that.

To go a step further, my friend, it is worth noting that virtue can bind men together. Have you ever considered that? Most men don't, I suppose. But virtue can take two men who share that virtue and it can hold them together in such a way and for such a purpose and with such strength that you would think they are brothers—or closer.

This gets me to thinking about some of the men that my grandfather used to speak about that he knew over in France. That was a bad time, to be sure—I think you all know about that, and I suppose folks have gotten to tellin' stories about it.

If they haven't yet, I reckon they will.

Anyhow, Granddaddy used to talk about the men he knew, and there were certain virtues they shared, at least to a point, and those men wound up finding out that they were bound together in ways that they could never have expected. They wound up closer than brothers. I suppose that blood has a way of doing that. Blood on the outside of a man has a unifying quality that blood on the inside of a man sometimes doesn't even dream. Isn't that strange? Sure it is, but you can better believe it is the truth.

So virtue binds men together, then, and there is something, you might say, *permanent* about that. Permanence is a rare commodity these days, and permanence sings a song that is beloved of the heart of man. If it lasts, it is something very real. There can be lapses, there can be periods of drought, and there can be entire fallings-out, but if it is true and if it is a real bond of virtue, then it persists.

I got to thinking about this just before everything changed, for I had been thinking about a man named John who went before some of us. John was a fairly old man, and a soft-spoken one at that. I only knew him in his understated dignity. Have you known men like that? Men who never attempt to stand out in the crowd, even if they have abilities or accomplishments that would make them stand out in any crowd. The kind of men who just go about doing what they need to do.

I was walking through a big, big store one day about six months before everything changed, and I ran into a very small, very old man who had a distinctive patch on his baseball cap, along with embroidery that identified him as a veteran of the Second World War. I found myself drawn to him and in a moment I was speaking with this dear, quiet man. Had he been in the particular airborne unit denoted on his hat? Yes, indeed he had. Had he jumped into Europe during the war? Again, indeed, he had. As it turned out, this dear quiet man had fought in a trying, trying place known as Bastogne. Yes, of course you know about it. The Battle of the Bulge. This dear, quiet man had carried a rifle and shot at Nazis and watched as his best buddy was shot and died in the foxhole right next to him. His eyes grew moist as he told me that.

I thanked the dear, quiet man for having served and for having put his life on the line and for losing so much for all of us—at that time yet unborn. He smiled at me, and with a distant, distant look said, "We were just doin' what we had to do."

I held my tears until I got to my car in the parking lot, and then I sat there for quite some time and cried. I cried for this man and for his goodness, and I cried for the buddy he lost that winter so long ago, and I cried for the virtue that joined these men together. That is some strong virtue, to be sure, so maybe now you get some idea of what it is that I'm talking about when I speak of virtue and when I speak of that bond. It is, I suppose, a bond that even death cannot break.

◆　◆　◆

So like I was saying when I started out, that sourwood was evergreen. It was placed right there as an emblem of eternal life and some kind of a hope in rebirth, but it is always kind of a crapshoot, when you come down to it, isn't it? I mean, there was a man who once said that faith was the membership card, or that faith was the key to the private washroom. Well, there is a sense in which that is the case, but I think more importantly that faith is what is going to get you by in times like those times when someone is laying a sprig of sourwood down in a place where you can see it—and some folks believe that it stands for something, and other folks just don't. That is just the way it is with people, as we are all so very different and you cannot force faith upon any man.

Just as well. I suppose if you could, then that faith wouldn't mean a whole hell of a lot.

Water Knot

(as told by Ashley, again)

Preston sat down, that fool Preston. He had such a big head, and I ain't talking full of himself, either. He had a big head, and I wouldn't have been surprised if he had to go and get the necks of his shirts enlarged just to get them over that big old head of his. Sometimes I thought something was wrong with him, if you know what I mean. Didn't that one lady from the health department show us all those pictures of the people, it was in Africa I think, that had big old heads? Maybe it was their stomachs that were big, or their feet, but I thought it was their heads...I don't know, I ain't sure. But anyhow there was something not right about those folks, and I always kinda felt deep down that maybe Preston was kind of the same. There was something just not right about him and his big old head...but the big old head was just the start of it.

So he sat down, and folks stared at him and that big old head of his, but those folk who got distracted got distracted by something pretty bad—it was something else and it sure as hell wasn't his head. He was holding that thing, right there in his hand, and he was smiling at it. And you just know that when Preston smiled, he smiled big. That smile stretched right across that big old face of his, and his face seemed even bigger than his head, if that's possible—I know it ain't, but it just seemed that way when he smiled.

So he sat down there and was lookin' at it layin' in his hand—only a little bloody—and when folks drew nearer to look at it, well, like I said, they kinda stopped payin' so much attention to his head and they started lookin' at it lyin' there in his hand. Again, like I said, it was only a little bloody, and folks thought it either woulda been bloodier or maybe they thought that Preston that fool just might have washed it off a little bit, but it wasn't really wet or nothin' either. It looked like it might still be warm.

That one guy who works at the garage in Cotton City was there that day, and he had enough guts to say, "Preston you fool, where'd you get that?" like Preston was gonna just answer and tell him where he done got it. We all figured he cut it off of someone, but no one was sayin' a thing, 'cause we didn't know whose it was, and well, if you cut it off someone then she'd probably hafta not be doin' so good and maybe even dead. 'Course we didn't want to say that, but it was what everyone was thinking. So the guy from the garage just said it and made it sound like Preston just found it lyin' around somewhere—like you find those things just lyin' around. 'Cause hell, you don't just go findin' things like that lyin' around, you know what I mean? The way you find spare change or maybe a cigarette butt that still's got some smokin' in it.

My brother Evan found a bottle with what he thought was whiskey in it, and that's what his friends told him, but when he tried it, well, it turned out someone had pissed in the bottle and Evan got sick.

There was that time that someone found what looked like a dried up eyeball over in Pole Creek near the septic tank outside of the rendering plant, but it turned out just to be some kind of tiny fruit that was just lyin' around. We didn't know.

Dang.

So Preston just sat there and kept on smilin' at it and holdin' it, and we all kind of kept quiet until The Sheriff showed up and helped Preston and his big old head into the patrol car and drove him away. Preston was back at work the next day, and he never said much about it, but he was always a little funny anyway, big head and all. The one lady at the dry-goods store—that would be Danny Lyman's mother's step-sister's friend—she walked with a limp and wore a heavy coat for the next few months and even in the heat of summer, so we all kind of wondered, but we never did ask and no one ever did offer. When she stopped limpin' and took the coat off and was normal and everything, some got to wonderin' again, but most just forgot about it.

Dang.

From Beyond the Grave

Reprise

It was a small thing, now that I look back at it, and I try not to look back at it very often. The way the end came was fairly unimportant, and I suppose it was the final joke in many ways. The man who brought me to my end is suffering a great deal more now, and I think that is always how it is. The one who has to go on through the rest of his life remembering some iniquity—large or small—at times pays a greater price than the victim. I am not siding with the criminal or the one in the wrong, mind you—I am just pointing out that the man who did it has gone on with his life but bears the weight of my death around his neck.

I am free. He, as it were, is encumbered.

To be free is a blessed, blessed thing—the sort of thing that a lot of people dream about, but a whole awful lot of people never really get to experience, as they find themselves bound to one thing or another. And you know, those things don't have to be the usual things that you think them to be, and in fact I suppose that most times they are not. It might seem almost a little silly, but there was that one preacher in Haverland when I was growing up, and he was bound ever so tightly to something that nearly became a cause of scandal. No, it wasn't any the things that you might think of, and it sure wasn't any of the things that they like to write about in the newspapers. In fact, it was so rather mundane that it never really even made the papers, but to the preacher it made him a prisoner all the same as if he had been tied up with a lady of the evening up in Cotton City or if he had been bound to the bottle. You see, that preacher had such a love for fried chicken that he didn't hardly have control over the stuff. He wasn't a big old man, neither—just pretty normal sized, but he had a voracious appetite, and when it came to a mess of fried chicken, there wasn't hardly a thing he could do to resist. Hell, he didn't even try to resist—he just gave right in and got himself wrapped right in the goodness of the stuff, and to him and to his "discipline" as he called it, that was the same as if he had been addicted to methamphetamine or the bottle or the scent of a bordello.

So you really couldn't say that the preacher was "free," because he sure was a prisoner to at least one thing. Hell, he mighta been a prisoner to more than that, but I only knew about the fried chicken, and I always thought it made a good example of what I'm talking about with this.

So the one who is beyond the condemnation or who is beyond the tragedy, well, I would just have to say that he or she is the one who is free, and in this case, the one responsible for the whole of it (while he thought he was freed by the action) has wound up being the one who is tied to the consequences until such time as perhaps death might grant him blessed release, and God willing, freedom.

I hope I haven't just got you all entirely confused by this. It would normally be at such a juncture in a conversation such as this that I might suggest a nice glass of sweet tea or maybe something a little bit stronger. However, considering the circumstances and the surroundings, I will have to just ask you to be content with our conversation. I do appreciate it.

Pistons and Dust

I just want it to go away and I almost can't think of it anymore. The dust has just got to get washed away, along with all the memories and the feelings and the horror and the hatred and the loathing and the dry, dry dusty place that the place of the dead sometimes is and the way that things look in the sunlight on a bright day in Crawford County. Things look different everywhere you go, you know, and the County is the same. Stuff has its own look. People have their own look. And when those people are away from there, maybe they look different as well. For if you take something out of its context—out of its own life-space—well, maybe you just take something of that thing away, too. Life and spaces and places and things and people are funny that way, don't you think?

So I want it all to end, I want it all to go away, I want it all to dry up even more than it already is, and I want it to blow away so as not to trouble the hearts of the faithful anymore. Blow away. Blow away, all you memories, all you pain, all you things that can hold a man back from living the way his Creator intended, and that the man himself wants to give in to and just dwell on and fester like a great, infected wound that allows its dirty, dirty pus and infected fluids to drain out of, all over the whole of things that are clean and healthy. For then that which is healthy gets infected as well, and the whole mess is just messed right up, as my Daddy used to say. Messed right up. And that's what happens.

I know that if I turn off the lights that nothing goes away, but yet to the person observing, it always seems like nothing is there anymore. Hell, you can't see it, of course. But to that which sees in darkness, everything is still right there—just the same, takin' up the same space, smellin' the same, lookin' the same, feelin' the same. Hell, if you can taste it, I know it would even taste the same. You gotta at least hand it all something for consistency, I would say, except when that is the very last thing you want, well, you still get it. Nothing changes in that regard. The blessing and the curse.

Orphan? Who is an orphan? Are we not all orphans, looking to get back to our parent and finding ourselves most days unable to even identify our mother, identify our father. That is just how it is, and it ain't never gonna change until, I suppose, until we draw our final breath. That man they used to call the theologian used to say that we would recognize the face, but not before he recognized us, as he always knows us. Well, I would expect a father or a mother or even an aunt or an uncle with custody to somehow recognize the face of the charge, wouldn't you? But as orphans, we just have to go about the business of trying to see the handprint or the fingerprint or the footprint of our parent in the dusty hood of that beat-up old sedan we call the soul.

So, sure as hell, I just want it to go away and I almost can't think of it anymore. The County, or rather the memory of The County screams at me and the memory of the people of that County and all the parts that keep hangin' on in my memory . . . all those things just scream as loud as you can imagine a silent scream bein' inside of your heart and inside of your soul. I just want it gone and I want it gone yesterday.

Where it goes, I cannot say. Where it sleeps, I cannot envision. It will go there and sleep and see itself refreshed, and all the world might look upon it with a favorable eye, knowing that the energy it gives in sleeping might far exceed the energy it gives in just standing still—I don't know, maybe just standing still and living the way that it really wants to live. Funny how it works out that way.

Postlude

I

It never seemed so real and yet it never seemed so far away and make-believe, in the sort of way that a different world that you learn about in a novel or a movie or a folk tale seems so far away and make-believe. Crawford County always did and forever will seem more real than any place in which I shall ever set foot, for a place where your heart has lived will always seem more like home than any other. I could live in another place for another lifetime and live and love and move and entirely have my being and yet it might not ever approach the way in which my heart has lived and died a hundred thousand times in that dry and dusty corner of that beloved land—a beloved land that offers herself up and promises to serve as both priest and victim and from time to time as the goddess herself. Why I ever hesitate to serve at her altar I shall never know, but I shall always regret. Always regret.

It never felt like a dream in the way that dreams have that other-than-perfect sort of feel, for Crawford County always felt like the perfect place to be and the perfect place to live a life that needed to be lived and feel perfect. For a man who was certainly not perfect nor who shall ever be perfect on this side of the Heavenly realm, a place that was as perfect as Heaven itself could never be recognized while one was living there, and it took separation from that Heaven on earth to let me know that it was something for which I been searching all my life.

And yet, when one's time in Heaven has run its due course, and the sinner looks upon those golden streets with the world-wise and world-weary gaze meant only for earthly vistas, well, I guess it is then that the sinner and Heaven alike need to come to a place of agreement. Most often, Heaven stays right where she is, and the sinner just moves along. Move along, sinner.

My eyes continue to spring open for the gathering of Heavenly light and my ears strain to hear the golden harps, playing lightly and falling sweetly upon ears that were never meant to hear such melody. And then I realize that Crawford County is gone and I can never go back, no matter how much I might like to erase the things I thought about how I wanted it to go away in the first place—along with the inbred knowing and the inbred showing and the inbred death and the inbred dying—such vile things that were and are inbred and in permanence built into the very DNA of those who inhabit those golden streets and those Heavenly courts and those gentle byways and those dusty crossroads and the quiet, quiet, quiet and sad pea fields sitting still and holding court for the cherubim and the seraphim and the school kids living that everlasting summer vacation and swinging on a rope taking them far out over the deep water in that swimming hole—because that swimming hole out back of Old Man So-and-So's barn is sometimes a lot deeper than you really think it is, and that rope swings you a lot farther out there than you ever expect, and then when the small and scrawny pale kid with the dark and protuberant mole on his neck screams with a raw, raw, vile scream and you all look up to realize that he held on a little too long and let go at the wrong time and has thus placed his frail, mortal body in very real and imminent danger, well, it is those times that you get to thinking that even if there were a time when you wanted this place called Heaven to go away you might never get your wish in a hundred lifetimes but in a heartbeat the chance might come like a thief in the night—just as the Master said. Broken bones and broken flesh and bruised memories are stock in trade but ever so surprising still in those Heavenly courts.

II

I know it seems like there is a lot of blood sometimes, but then you start to realize how much blood each one of us carries around with us in our bodies. It is an awful lot when you have to clean it up, but it is precious little when there is no ambulance to take a broken and torn body to Cotton City. Cotton City. I still say that name as though the place exists outside of the four walls of my mind and my memories and my heart, and I look upon those memories of that place with disdain in the same sort of way I looked with disdain upon Cotton City herself. There are better things to waste your time despising and disdaining than places. Maybe one could even use that energy in hating the people who live in those places, or maybe not. Some places are just not worth the hating, and so it is with the folks who live there—they just are not worth the hating and the hating eats up the hater, and not the hated, so in the end we are just better off having the places and the people stay the way they are and not really even raise up their heads. If you don't stick your head up over the edge of the trench, you won't get it shot off, or so my granddad used to say, up until the time he died. I think he knew the truth of that firsthand.

Firsthand knowing is funny that way, you know. Just now I can somewhat recall the death of an old, old soldier, who died and was laid to rest with his brothers in arms. I guess that if anyone knows what that sort of life is like, it is an old, old soldier. This soldier, he had lived so much longer than any of his comrades, so much so that they were all gone when he was an old, old man, and he had no one else to talk to about the war, except a handful of historians who cared enough about it to talk to him. Sadly, when he spoke of the trenches and the wire and the gas and the blood and the body parts hanging up in the limbs of what used to be trees before the shells tore them apart, everyone just smiled or grimaced or shook their heads but they didn't know. No. Not at all. And they just couldn't understand. And so when we all said goodbye to that old, old soldier, it was the closing of a chapter. The closing of a book. But to everyone on the outside—the outside of his life (who was all of us)—it was just a book of fiction. But the trenches and the wire and the gas and the blood and the body parts, well, hell, that was no fiction.

And so my firsthand knowing of Crawford County seemed just like a combination of that old, old soldier's understanding of the war and the denial or the shock or the disbelief that everyone else had about it.

My own granddad didn't make it as far as that old soldier, but I knew he knew it firsthand as well. He was quiet and never said a word. Winding on those long strips of wool they called "puttees" every Memorial Day to march with his old veteran friends in the parade. So proud and so sweaty but the heat never got to those old men who would salute the colors and never mind that they were just an elderly footnote to the veterans of "the Big One." Now they're all gone.

So it was like that, or it is like that, with Crawford County. You get to know something, no matter how real it is or no matter how real or false the passing of time and your memory make it. It just gets to be so that when you know it firsthand you just know it and there is nothing that is going to change the way you know it. It kind of reminds me about the story of that man in the old Soviet Union who had the photos changed to show only what he wanted—he had it done to the point that one other man was absolutely taken out of a photograph and of course no one really knew that they had done that. They just assumed it had always been so and that the picture was just as it had come out of the camera. Those who knew better knew what they had done and there were even some who tried to set the record straight. Record-straightening seldom works, you know. And the more you try to straighten in any one given place, well, you just know that it is going to get even more and more crooked in another. That is just how it is and I can't change it.

III

And so it closes. Or I might say, "and so it draws to a close." Either way you know what I'm talking about. Maybe someone drew it shut. Maybe it just shut up on its own. Any old way you slice it, it comes up shut. Ain't open no more. Closed.

The darkest thing you ever done seen is so dark, and the brightest thing, in comparison, well, hell it could nearly blind a man. I just keep thinking, when I get myself to thinking about Crawford County, well I keep hearing and thinking those words "more light" as though it were a plea, or a prayer or just some sort of simple request. But in any way you look at it, that most simple and heartfelt desire for more light is really at the heart of our need and at the very heart of who we are—we want to dwell in the light—seein' as how the light is where it's safe and where we have some sense of what is going on. In the dark, we don't. Some men will go their whole lives in the dark—some hoping for and desiring the light, and yet others having no desire for the light as they have no idea that there is anything else aside from the darkness they live in. The saddest of all are those men who live in the dark and can see the light but they have no desire for the light themselves, because they don't want to see how filthy and dirty the little corners of their lives are when the light goes shining in there. It's kind of like when you drop a screw or a coin or a button or something and the danged thing takes a bounce and then goes rollin' under the couch or the dry sink or something. Naturally, you go and stoop on down and look for it, and if you actually go and shine a flashlight, well, you just can't stomach to look under there—it bein' so dusty and dirty and all. Well, our lives are like that, and it really takes shining a light into our lives for us to see it. Some men can't see, and some men just don't want to.

Crawford County is always there, maybe. For, yes, I believe it is—always hidden, always just around the corner, always just through the thin veil of reality. It is there and while unseen it shall remain more real than anything. And I shall always find myself together with those who walk those dusty lanes and who feel the stony, rocky paths beneath their feet, bruising heel and wearying the step with dust. And remembering all the time that if the rocks in this place could talk, they'd tell you to ask the trees. And reminding you that if the trees in this place could talk, they'd tell you to ask the wind. And if the wind could talk, well, maybe it just might tell you exactly what you'd expect it to say. And those souls that the wind speaks of, well they are together forever. For what virtue has united, death can *never* separate. And for such a gift, we are never worthy.

PART II

Wild Torrent

I

Blind Charles put the severed finger in his mouth and I watched him do it. There was some kind of dirt stuck to it, as you might expect from a severed finger that you would find lyin' there on the ground like some kind of cast-off jalapeno pepper or something, except that you knew it was not just something that fell off of a pepper plant, but rather had started its life as a tiny little curled up finger, looking for all the world like a cocktail shrimp, and part of a whole set of them on a little tiny baby. By the time that Blind Charles put the damned thing in his mouth you would have never guessed that it ever had such a sweet and innocent origin—a genesis, as it were. The beginnings of things were always a lot more innocent than the endings, it seemed, and so it was with this tiny little curled up finger, taken from a hand that would have seemed surprised to suddenly be in possession of one less of its digits— could that a hand be surprised in the way the whole person is.

◆ ◆ ◆

We were all working on the Dempseys' farm. The Dempseys had been farming that land for a long time, and we all knew the family pretty well. The Dempsey kids had gone to school with all of us in town, and Mr. Dempsey, seeing as how he had one of the biggest farms in the whole area, well he was always keen to give some work to guys who couldn't find it anywhere else. A few of us, me included, were regular seasonal help, and I was even lucky enough to work for Mr. Dempsey over most winters too, as I more or less knew my way around a lot of different kinds of farm machinery and I was pretty careful about the way I worked and Mr. Dempsey always said he liked that. He was big on safety at his farm, and most of us couldn't really remember a time when there was a bad accident at his place.

They say that farms are the most dangerous workplaces in America, especially for the young, and I mostly believe that to be true. While Dempsey's was pretty safe, there had been something pretty bad over at the Austin farm a few years back and I think that everybody working on the farms in the whole county probably kept that in the back of their mind. It seems that Old Man Austin's nephew Jared had been working with a brush chipper—not strictly farm machinery, I guess, but it was on the farm. Jared had been working with a few other guys, clearing brush out of a little plot of land that they had just begun to clear, and he was running one of them old-style brush chippers—it was one without a kill switch built in as a safety. The new ones pretty much all have some kind or other of a brake bar built in around the feed throat of the chipper. That way, if you're throwing brush into the throat and for some dumb reason you hold on to the brush or the sticks, well, before you can be pulled into the grinder itself part of your body bumps the big old bar that runs across the throat, and the machine stops instantly.

As I said, the chipper that Jared was using was old—it was a lot older than Jared himself, in fact, and it sure as hell didn't have any sort of a kill switch like that. Ricky Pillman, the big, bald headed farm hand with the cracked tooth in front would always try to scare people by saying that he saw a chipper like that turn a man's "skull into cinders in three seconds." We would all just kind of look down when he repeated that more than a few times each season, but it was probably true. A lot of folks just didn't like to be reminded of things like that. I guess it would be because each one of us has a skull, and not a single one of us like the thought of it being reduced to cinders. It kind of bothers a guy that way, I suppose.

Well, as it was, Jared was helping to clear the brush off a plot of land, and it was getting near the end of a day. Jared and everybody else was tired, and you probably know how it can be when you are supposed to concentrate on something but you're just so danged tired that you can't really keep your mind in one place. I've been so tired a few times that I don't know that I could have said the alphabet the right way if you would have asked me to. Jared was getting tired, and everybody that was working with him that day says that they were too. Well, Jared kind of lost his concentration, and the guys said they saw him look away for just a bit and either his glove or his sleeve got caught on a branch, they suppose, and the next thing you know Jared was screaming his head off. He got pulled into that thing so damn quick, and it took his arm in past the elbow and half way up to his shoulder. Somehow it kind of jammed and the engine shut down or one of the guys hit the kill switch or Jared did—no one really remembers the details over the screaming and the blood.

Well, Jared was stuck in that thing with his arm two-thirds gone and they say he just got pale and passed out as they were trying to free him from it. They finally got his arm out of the chipper, but they said he was gone by that time. The doctor said it was likely shock and blood loss. Old Man Austin felt somehow to blame, and things were never the same between him and Jared's dad—that would be Old Man Austin's brother. And the upshot of all of it was that folks around these parts seemed to keep that in mind and farm owners were always going on about safety with the hired help—more than they ever had before.

◆ ◆ ◆

The finger had been lyin' there on the ground for just a moment, but sometimes when people act in crazy ways they act quickly and they act in such a spontaneous manner. So it was with Blind Charles, and we all knew it. The moment that the finger was on the ground we all just stopped and held our breath—in that ignisecond (as Cousin Stevie called it) wherein you just don't know what to do. There is a pause in the life of each of us that could be used for all sorts of things, all sorts of decisions. Lots of folks get that pause on a regular basis, it seems, whereas I suppose that most of us just don't really get that pause except for maybe a time or two in the course of our life. That pause where the heart and the mind might be at odds and the soul or the spirit or whatever you want to call it is just coming along for the ride. Heart and mind lock themselves in some kind of a wrestling match, tearing at each others' throats and even trying to pull hair and gouge eyes if you really get down to it. They might even kick in the shins and worse places, if you think about it.

So there was that pause, and there was that blink, and there was even some kind of a collective intake of breath amongst the few of us standing around. One of us even made a sound you could hear right aloud, but that was nothing compared to the way in which the silence was broken in just a minute. We stopped. We looked. Bitter, who had just lost the finger, turned white. I've never seen anyone really turn white, before or since, but Bitter turned white. I thought for a second that he was going to pass out, but he just stood there in the sun, wavering from side to side a little bit, and then he looked down at his hand.

The silence after that collective intake of breath was deafening, like I heard someone say once about a silence, but this one really was. We all stood, for the second half of that quiet moment, looking at the finger on the ground, corn stubble and sawdust and farmyard dirt all kind of mixed together, a boot print over boot prints over ground-up cigarette butts. The typical things you find there in a farmyard where men are working and men are cussing and men are smoking. You find severed fingers in the mix only if you are in places where men are losing fingers, strangely enough. This was not originally supposed to be one of those places, I would suppose, but then no one ever expects to have folks losing fingers in any place. Who would want to?

Before anyone could say anything, we were all catapulted into a dream that was even stranger and felt less real than what we all had just been in. One moment we were working with a stubborn baler, the next moment Bitter sees his finger get caught under wire in the machinery somehow, and the next moment after that Blind Charles is putting the finger in his mouth.

Now Blind Charles wasn't blind, it needs be said. Blind Charles was just called that on account of the thick glasses he had worn since anyone can remember him being around—ever since he was a little kid he had those big old thick lenses perched up on his nose, making his eyes look all kind of big and strange. Years later I saw pictures of him as a real little shaver, and you could only guess that those same old glasses were perched up on his nose—it was as if he had the very same style of eyeglasses for the past thirty or so years, maybe forty. Who knows? They looked identical, and Blind Charles was just Blind Charles to all of us, but he had never really done anything strange or out of the ordinary. He had never popped a severed finger into his mouth before, so this all took us a little by surprise.

When he put the finger in his mouth, he didn't really even stop to consider it, and I think that was what caught us all off guard. He just reached right down, straining a bit to bend at the waist, on account of that gut of his. Stevie used to say that it looked like Blind Charles had a small sheep strapped to his stomach, right under his shirt, that he just wore it for warmth or companionship or whatever, but we all knew from right early on that it was just a joke, and that Blind Charles was just a little overweight—it wasn't a sheep. So he strained a bit to bend over at the waist, but he just reached right down and plucked that finger off the ground. It was like he didn't even stop to think about it—like he had been standing at a picnic and someone had a plate of sliced raw vegetables just sitting there on the table. Celery, broccoli, black olives, carrots, maybe some sliced mushrooms. Right in the center, of course, you would have a little dish or a plastic container full of ranch dressing or maybe a dill dressing—the kind that goes with raw vegetables. It was like Blind Charles had been standing there, just munching on the raw vegetables and it just so happened that suddenly there was a carrot in the dish that looked like a severed finger. Hell, it even had a little bit of dirt on it, so it maybe just looked like a really fresh baby carrot that hadn't yet been washed or peeled. And so Blind Charles just bent over as natural as could be, selected this nice, fresh, unwashed baby carrot in the form of a severed human finger, picked it right up and without even really looking at it, he put it in his mouth.

There was, again, just a moment of silence when we all stood there and looked at Blind Charles. I, for one, expected him to do one of two things, I guess. I thought he might spit it right out, or I thought he might start chewing. I mean, what do you really expect when someone puts someone else's severed finger in his mouth?

"Give me my finger," said Bitter, with a look of disbelief on his face. He was more concerned about the whereabouts of his missing finger in that moment than he was about the blood running out of his hand. I reached for a rag and pressed it against Bitter's stump. He jumped back, looked at me like I was the one who cut the finger off, and then came to his mind, grabbed the rag, and pressed it against where his finger had been. He looked almost crazed—half in anger, half in disbelief. The anger was mostly, I suppose, at the baling machine or at himself for getting his little finger in there. I don't know, maybe there was some anger in there toward Blind Charles, but I got the impression that it was mostly disbelief that Bitter was showing to Blind Charles just at that moment.

In the moment that we all looked at the finger, it was like slow-motion as it made its way into his mouth. I saw the bluish-purple rim around the red and white stump—most patriotic, I thought. Bone always reminds me of dressing out game—anytime I see the white of bone and tendon it reminds me of dressing out game. And game it was, I suppose, at least to some of the folk who were watching and some of us who were, as I said, staring in disbelief at the whole episode.

"Give me my finger," said Bitter again, taking a step toward Blind Charles. Bitter was pressing the rag against the stump or against the very base of the joint, actually, and he didn't make any threatening moves at all. He just walked the couple of steps across the farmyard toward Blind Charles, but he did so with determination and a look on his face—a lot like a man who was trying to recover his car keys from a service desk or a coat from a hat-check room. It was odd, as though it really wasn't all that urgent, and Bitter never let on at that point that he was the least bit concerned about getting his finger back. He seemed to be concerned, for sure, but I suppose he could have had no doubt that the finger would end up on his hand again.

"Give Bitter his finger, Charles," said Topher, the oldest hand on our crew. He had been in the Army and he seemed to always have a really level head on him no matter what happened. This was trying his intellectual and emotional maturity, though, I suppose, as it was for all of us. I don't think a single one of us knew anything different than that we just wanted Blind Charles to give Bitter back his finger, but not one of us had the least bit idea of how we were going to see that come to pass.

Blind Charles stretched himself up to his full height, pursed his lips, and then took in a long breath through his nostrils. He appeared as though he was about to speak, and again there was a long pause. Charles looked up into the sky, like he was looking a good distance off, and all at once he started pushing that severed finger of Bitter's out through his pursed lips. He had turned the thing around in his mouth, because we all saw it go in with the fingertip first, and we saw that awfully patriotic raw stump end go in last, but he started pushing it out with the fingertip leading the way—all the more awful, I thought, as he would have to be pushing on the raw, bloody stump end with his tongue to make it come out. But I guess that if you don't mind putting some other guy's severed finger in your mouth, then you don't really mind pushing on the raw stump end with your tongue. It takes a special guy in either case.

Everyone stared in silence as Blind Charles stood there like a wooden Indian statue outside of a tobacco store or a barber shop, with his right hand raised up perfectly straight and flat out in front of him at shoulder height, as if to say, "How," like the old tobacco store Indians would do. He stood there with his hand up, and I think we all thought he was just trying to say "stop" or "halt," as if he thought we were going to advance on him and maybe try to take his prize finger away from him. It was weird.

"Charles, that finger don't belong to you—that's Bitter's finger," said Topher, moving a little closer to Charles despite the warning that he held out for all of us. "You just give that here, 'cause we can get Bitter and his finger to a doctor in the city, and they can reattach that finger, like I seen them do on TV. I know they can, so just give it over."

Charles, still standing there, let his lips break from their tight, pursed grip around Bitter's finger, and slide right into the most playful looking grin you ever did see. He started laughing through his nose and around the finger, and his belly moved with every breath. He still said nothing, and it was as if he wasn't really looking at anyone in particular. Through the thick lenses of his glasses, we could tell that he was still looking off over the fields and off toward the horizon. He looked a little bit like he was trying to remember something—trying to remember a place he had been, something that someone had said, or almost as though he was trying to remember the words to a part he was playing in a stage play. Sometimes, though, I feel just like that, and I suppose we all kind of take that approach to life, and just try to remember the lines we wish we had the foresight to learn.

When Blind Charles started laughing it seemed to startle everyone a little bit, especially Bitter. "Stop it," he cried out, "stop your damn laughing and give me my damned finger now, Charles."

Everyone joined in shouting at Blind Charles and screaming at him to give back Bitter's finger, but it didn't seem to move Charles the least bit. He stood there, laughing and holding that finger between his teeth and lips like a cigar or more like a wilted piece of pale asparagus, but still with the farm dirt under the fingernail.

Bitter dove at Blind Charles, hitting him squarely in the mid-section and toppling the big guy over into the dirt and the corn stubble. Everyone else dove right on in, and for a second it wasn't sure what the intention was—no one was sure if the more pressing need was going to be getting Bitter's finger out of Blind Charles's mouth or keeping Bitter from killing Blind Charles. It was most likely a combination of the two, but as soon as Bitter's good hand took a swipe at trying to grab his finger out of Charles's mouth, well, Charles just popped that finger right back in, and stopped his laughing. Bitter drew his hand back again and took an open-palmed slap at Charles, who turned red in an instant. Bitter then grabbed at Charles's jaw, and tried forcing open his mouth. He climbed right on top of him and tried forcing his thumbs into the corners of Blind Charles's mouth, smearing blood on the one side of Charles's head with the bloody stump of his. Everyone was shouting. Topher realized that things were getting bad.

"Bitter, take it easy on him . . . Charles, give him back his finger you damned fool! Come on the both of you, just stop it . . . this is crazy," Topher shouted at them, and you could see that he was getting sweatier than he already had been from the work—he was getting nervous and everyone was coming a little unglued. The shouting kept getting louder, and everyone started getting physical with the two of them. Some of us were pulling on Bitter, trying to get him off of Charles's chest and trying to wrench his hands away from his mouth, others were trying to open Charles's mouth themselves, pushing on his cheeks, trying to wedge their fingers between his upper and lower sets of molars right through his stubbly cheeks. Nothing was working and Charles was getting really red in the face, causing me to worry that he might not be in control of his actions, like he was sick or that he was having a seizure or something. It was awful.

Sometimes people will say things like "It's the calm before the storm," or you hear them talk about a tornado coming and they say something like "It always gets real quiet and still 'fore a twister hits." Now I don't know if there really is any truth to all of that, but there is sometimes something like that which plays out with folks. It is like maybe the old sayings about the weather have a lot more to do with the way people act and the way people live and love and die and eat their cornbread than they even do about the way the weather plays it. So it was kind of like it that day when Blind Charles picked up Bitter's severed finger just like it was a raw vegetable off a tray before dinner, and put that severed finger into his mouth. All hell broke loose and the guys were climbing all over the two of them when they were wrestling on the ground, fighting for that finger.

All the shouting and the wrenching around and the slapping and the grappling just got real still and no one said a word. I thought for a second that Blind Charles had dropped the finger and the whole thing was going to come to an end and we were going to have to think about how we were going to get Bitter to the hospital in the city the quickest way possible, when the smoke, as it were, cleared, the guys all rolled away from Blind Charles who was on his back with his head craned back and his mouth held wide open, and Bitter's finger nowhere in sight.

II

"He swallowed my finger! He swallowed it!" Bitter was out of his mind and you would have sworn to yourself that if he had a knife in his hand right then he would have gutted Blind Charles right straight open and left him to bleed out, just lying there in the farmyard. Bitter, you could just imagine, would stand there with the knife in his hand, looking at Blind Charles just lying there on his back with his abdomen all sliced open and more blood than anyone should ever see in one place, and Bitter would have a knife in one hand and his little finger in the other, holding it like a prize that he won at the fair. We could all see that, I am sure, in what Mr. Tanner, my English teacher in school, used to call "the mind's eye," but as it turned out, we didn't get to really see any of it. If Bitter had a mind to cut Blind Charles open, he never acted on it, and even though Bitter tried taking a few swings at him, everyone saw best to just hold him back. Blind Charles had just swallowed another man's finger, and he was lying there with his jaw still hanging open and his head all tilted back, eyes looking up at the pure blue sky—a sky that matched Blind Charles's eyes almost perfectly, as well as the blue cotton shirt that he wore, now stained here and there with the spatterdash marks of Bitter's blood that grew darker by the minute. My Aunt Dahlia would have cautioned him to get some cold water on those stains right away, lest they set up.

There are times when the bluest sky over the farm fields can make it seem as though there isn't a single thing wrong in the world. Perfect summer days when the air is cool in the morning and the heat of day hasn't made it unbearable yet, and the sky is just that perfect, perfect shade of blue, like a cotton shirt or like that perfect blue baby blanket that I remember used to hang on the wash line of that family down the street from us—the family that had all the children and Daddy said they were Catholic and so they had a lot of children because they had to and so the blue baby blanket got a fresh workout about every year, no matter if the new member of the household was girl or a boy. Perfect, perfect blue and a blue that spoke of fidelity and purity and hope and truth. But then you saw that same blue in a perfect blue sky right over a spot where men wanted to almost kill each other over craziness and that same blue reflected in the eyes of a crazy man that you always thought was sane and then you notice that the crazy man's shirt is the same color blue and so it might not always stand for purity or hope, leastaways.

Blind Charles stood up, and Bitter seemed to calm down for just a second, but when everyone had dropped their hold on anyone else, Bitter dove at Charles with his fist and delivered right to his stomach about the heaviest blow I ever seen. I think we all thought that Bitter was trying to get Charles to puke up the finger, but Charles just doubled over and grabbed his gut in pain as he fell to the dirt. Topher and me just grabbed Bitter again and I said that we had to get him to the doctor no matter what so that he didn't bleed to death or get some kind of infection. Everyone thought this was a good, sound plan of action, and so Topher and a couple others bundled Bitter into a truck and headed out to town, the wheels spinning and throwing a whole load of gravel in the air as they turned around and headed onto the blacktop. I walked over to Blind Charles.

Men who have made mistakes usually come to realize it before too long and sometimes the first reaction is to try to rationalize their actions. I don't know if this is what Charles was doing, but he started shaking his head back and forth real fast, his eyes reddening and kind of welling up with tears. It was uncertain if the tears were tears of remorse or tears of pain over the massive blow that Bitter had landed in his gut. Maybe it was a bit of both. Charles shook his head back and forth and looked at me with puffy eyes. "Denny," he said to me quietly, "what's going on?"

There are questions that you sometimes can't answer because they are too difficult to answer. I was asked once in school something about if it was possible that all of what we see was the only real stuff that was going on—you know, if what happens in the world is real only because someone is seeing it . . . like me or you and then you telling me about it because you saw it and so it was real, although what you saw and was real for you might not be as real for me because I was only hearing about it from someone who really did see it. And so this begged the question about if anything was real and maybe was nothing really there if no one was looking at it, and did maybe it all go away when we closed our eyes or went into the next room? We were taught that there was a thinker one time— some kind of famous smart guy in Europe, I think, who thought that this could really be the case and that what we saw was maybe all just like a dream and that somebody had to be seeing it for it to be real. This made us all kind of nervous, because if a man was intelligent to be a great thinker and get his ideas put into a book that they were using to teach in the schools, well maybe there was something to what he was saying, and I got real concerned that maybe things weren't as I thought they were—that maybe my house and my family and my dog and all my things were just things that I imagined and weren't really there. Maybe they all went away when I closed my eyes or slept or when I went down to the river and was away from my house and family. This bothered me like crazy.

The whole thing was resolved, I felt, for the most part, when my teacher said that this great European thinker's solution was that there had to be somebody who saw everything and therefore caused everything to exist all the time—not just when one of us was looking at it. This person who saw everything all of the time and in every place was God, or so my teacher said. God was everywhere and he could see everything and he never stopped looking all the time. As further proof of this, my teacher took a dollar bill out of his wallet and showed us the back with that pyramid with an eye atop the thing. This was what he called the "all seeing eye of God," and he assured us all that it never closed and it never slept, and therefore we were all real as could be because we dwelt in the mind of God, who made us as real as a cornfield and the river and the dirt. I felt a lot better after having it explained to me that way.

So if that was the sort of question that I couldn't answer because it was too difficult, there were other questions you just can't answer because you can't bear to tell the person asking what the answer is, and these are even harder yet. I have never really had to answer (or not answer, as it were) too many of these, but I saw Officer Preston try to give that kind of answer to Mr. Wallsworth the mechanic when his son had taken his own life and no one could really bear to give the news to him because the whole town knew that Mr. Wallsworth had just been diagnosed with a real bad cancer and was not long for this world. Everyone thought that Teddy, his son, had offed himself because he couldn't bear to see his dad die, even though that was a hell of a thing to do because his old man would have to deal with some of the consequences (and those all the while he was navigating his own last days here on this earth). It was awful, just awful. And I happened to be next door in their neighbor's garden trying to steal tomatoes off the vine, and I heard the whole thing. Officer Preston just could not bring himself to tell Mr. Wallsworth the truth and so he made up a story, the exact details of which I forgot, and when I read it in the news the next day I just remember looking right through the paper—figuratively as well as in real life. I sat for the longest time staring right through the paper and trying to put myself right in Officer Preston's shoes and the awful feeling in his gut he had to be feeling when he was trying to explain it. I realized I probably would have done the same thing, but I'm not nearly as smart as Officer Preston, so I would have screwed up the whole story and wound up saying dumb things. Thank God for smart guys like Officer Preston who know how to tell a story and make it sound true.

Mr. Wallsworth died about a week after the whole thing—Teddy was hardly in the grave a few hours when his dad checked into the hospital again and things just got worse and worse. And for the second time in about a week I found myself staring up at the sky while I was lying down in the grass in our backyard, and I was thinking again about what I did in a hard situation, although I started contemplating it from both sides this time. I thought about what Officer Preston had to have said, and the things he would have felt while he was telling them, but I also thought a good deal about Mr. Wallsworth and how he felt. I tried to imagine how my heart would have ached in either situation, and it was pure hell so I just gave up and went inside. My mom had just made a shoo-fly pie, and she asked if I wanted some with a cold glass of milk. You would have to be crazier than all get-out to turn down that beautiful, dark, and nearly holy taste of blackstrap molasses being washed down with a cold glass of fresh whole milk, so I stopped my thinking for the day.

So those were really the two types of questions that a man might find it hard to answer, and then there was the question that I was facing now from Blind Charles. "Denny," he had said to me, "what's going on?"

Sometimes you get a question that is hard or damned near impossible to answer not because it's difficult or because you can't bear to tell the answer. There are questions you can't bear to answer because you can't believe the question is being asked, and this was exactly that sort of question. How could Blind Charles not know what was going on? He had been in the center of all that had gone on this whole crazy morning, and I thought we both knew it. But still he looked at me with those puffy eyes and cheeks that could have stood a closer shaving and he nearly looked through me and he asked me what was going on. I don't think that I really did anything—I know I didn't say anything at first, and I think that I couldn't even shake my head. I mostly just listened to the wind blow and the sound of some bird singing nearby. I don't know the first thing about birds, and I certainly can't identify a bird by the song that it sings, but there was a bird singing and that is all that I remember.

"Going on?" I repeated eventually. "Going on? What the hell do you mean?"

"Denny, you see how blue those skies are, don't you?"

"Sure, Charles, I see it."

"Blue skies never hurt no one, do they, Denny?"

"What do you mean?"

"Just the skies alone. They don't hurt no one, do they? I mean, it's gotta be something else, right?"

"Charles," I said, "Bitter's finger done got cut off and you swallowed it." I figured the only way to get through this whole little bit of beating around the bush was going to be just getting right down to brass tacks as my Uncle Connie used to say. I never really knew what he meant by that, and he was an accountant, so I don't think he used a lot of tacks aside from in his bulletin board, but I knew that it meant to get down to business, and this I tried to do by just laying the facts out on the line for Blind Charles. He would either take it or leave it.

As it turned out, he *gave* something instead, and in the end it was like one of those gifts you're not really sure if you were glad that someone gave you or if you just wished they might have kept it for themselves or for someone else instead.

III

Blind Charles sat up and crossed his legs with some difficulty. His thighs were fat. Really fat, in fact, and his coveralls didn't fit too well in the legs—they were a little too short for him, and they were certainly too tight, or at least tighter than I would have wanted them.

"Denny," he said, "they're awfully blue. You remember the old brick school down near the edge of town?"

"Sure."

"Well, Denny, you know I used to live right near there when I was growing up, right?"

"Sure I do."

"It was a long time ago, Denny, or at least it seems like a long time ago. We were just kids. I suppose everyone is just a kid at least once in their life and when you are, there just some things you can't help doing. You know, like having zits and popping them in front of a mirror—I think 'most everyone does that at some point. Hell, I think the only girl I ever dated probably decided to never see me again after I kind of absentmindedly picked at a zit when we were out on a date. I squeezed at it without even really thinking and she said, 'Charles, please don't do that,' and I never did in her presence again, but not because I kept myself from doing it but because she never went out with me again. Never mind the fact that the zit was on my back and we were in a restaurant."

I tried to imagine this and stopped. Blind Charles continued.

"But zits are just something you go through when you're a kid, right? So are things like bad breath because you don't know that it's bad and you ain't learned about keeping yourself clean and no one has told you that maybe you need to chew a stick of gum or have a mint after you eat that bag of Funyons at lunch time. Life just ain't fair. So it seemed no worse when I saw Mahler and Pennick and those other kids that used to hang around together, and they were all hanging around on a summer night—all hanging around the playground at that old brick school down near the edge of town. They were lighting off firecrackers—I could hear them going off. I was sitting in my room reading a book, but I had the windows open because it was hot out, and I could hear the firecrackers and the laughing and every now and then someone cussing and then the laughing would get louder."

"Well," he continued, "it was sounding so fun I decided to put down my book and go see what was going on. It wasn't that late yet, and it was summer, so it was still light out and my mom didn't mind that I was going out of the house. I told her I was going to the playground and she just told me to be careful and to be back before it got dark. I wandered over to see who was there, even though I already knew."

Blind Charles paused for a moment, and we both just took in the skies and the fields. A big old bank of clouds moved in front of the sun, making a big shadow. Everything got a little darker, and it even got a little cooler, it seemed. I looked at my forearms and saw that goosebumps were rising up, so I ran my hands across them quickly. It was strange to feel goosebumps on such a warm summer day, but stranger was to look at Charles and his blue cotton shirt— the color of the blue changed as the cloud moved in front of the sun. It started out as bright blue as the skies themselves, but as the cloud moved the shirt looked darker and darker, and with it the blood smears. They looked for a moment almost black, but I think it was just my eyes. The shirt got to look like a dark gray or a blue that had been painted on a building in a place where they burned a lot of coal or some such thing, and it didn't match the skies anymore, even though the skies had been the exact same color just a moment ago. I looked even more intently at Charles and his blue eyes, which also had been the same color as the skies. Now it appeared as though their color didn't matter at all. His eyes just looked sadder, and they almost looked a little older than they had been. By the time Charles began talking again, the clouds had moved along and were going on their merry little way, and the shadows no longer cursed the blue of his shirt and his eyes.

"Pennick had a whole box full of firecrackers that his uncle had brought from somewhere that he was vacationing, and they were all having a great time putting those firecrackers into empty tin cans, blasting apart glass bottles, and digging little holes in the lawn of the schoolyard and seeing how much turf they could blow up in a single blast. I started watching even though they were none too polite to me and called me blind and four-eyes and all the usual crap I used to get called as a kid. Still do, sometimes. Did you know that, Denny?"

"Know what, Charles?"

"That people call me names. They always have. They call me all sorts of things, mostly to do with my eyes."

"We all get called names, Charles. It ain't nothing, really." I think I must have turned pretty red as I was saying this, because I had always called him Blind Charles and sometimes even worse. Charles was right, though, that folks had always called him names and it was mostly to do with his eyes.

"Well, after Mahler and Pennick and the others had blown up most of the stuff they could find laying around, one of the other kids goes looking around near the edge of the playground and pretty soon shouts out that he's found something pretty cool. We all ran over and there was a big black crow, all dead and looking kind of nasty. Mahler poked it with a long stick and proclaimed it really dead. We all figured that, anyway, though. Well, Pennick pulls out a big old firecracker and says they should blow its head off and how cool that would be. Everyone laughs and agrees, and then they turn to me. 'Hey four-eyes,' he said, 'you get to set the charge on the prisoner.' He pointed to the crow and then handed me the firecracker. I told him I didn't want to and that somebody else could have the honor. He asked me if I was some kind of a pussy and was there something wrong with me. The others started to laugh and I felt funny inside, so I said I'd do it. He handed me the firecracker and a cigarette lighter and they all ran a little ways away. To take cover."

Blind Charles looked even puffier around the eyes as he told this tale, and his voice sounded kind of dry and creaky. If I would have had some water I would have offered him a drink, but I didn't and so I just let him continue.

"I was scared, Denny. I never liked touching dead things—still don't. But the last thing I really wanted to look like was a pussy—scaredy-cat. So I kind of pried open the crow's beak with one hand and then jammed the firecracker in as far as I could with the other. I pushed on it a little more so that just the wick was sticking out. I felt like my fingers that had touched the crow were somehow unclean and that I was going to get a disease, but I didn't want to show I was afraid in front of the others so even though I really wanted to smell my fingers and then wipe them on the cool grass, I just kept at my work. It took me several tries to get the cigarette lighter going, seeing as how I didn't have a lot of experience using one of them. Finally the fuse lit and it sparked and sizzled while I held the crow's head in my other hand. I heard the other kids yelling to drop the crow and run, and I could hear others laughing at me, but I just stood there, staring down and looking at that crow with the firecracker in its mouth."

"That's awful, Charles," I said.

"Yeah, but Denny, when the firecracker went off, it was even worse yet. I thought my fingers had been blown off, and I got crow brains or something all on me—on my shirt and even some on my face. Whatever it was smelled just awful, and I remember still standing there and crying—screaming, and I could hear my mom shouting after me from our yard, as she must have heard my screaming and knowed it was me. She ran up to me and was shouting at the other kids, and saying how she was going to call their parents and the police and how they should all just go home and stop getting into trouble and disturbing the peace. And she put her arm around me and I remember stopping my crying just long enough to look down at the crow and seeing some sort of hideous, mangled bird head, and a blown-off, ragged little stump of a beak still in place on what was left of the crow's head, just looking at me like it was accusing me of something worse than killing him."

After he said that we both just sat there in silence and watched another cloud move in front of the sun.

IV

After hearing that story about the crow and the firecracker I didn't say anything. I looked out over the tops of the corn and thought about the trees in the distance and about the little river that they were all congregating around. I heard a guy talking about this once, and I think it might have been in school, but I'm not too sure. It could have been on some kind of documentary or something, or maybe just a little bit on a news show. A lot of times I can't remember where I saw or heard stuff, anyway.

This particular guy was saying something about the way that things congregate, and I don't think that he was thinking too far beyond what he was saying, but there certainly was room to understand what he said outside of that. It had something to do with trees all congregating around a river because that was where the water was, and so you could see that real easily when you were out driving across the open highway or something and you knew that a river was coming up by looking on your map. If you weren't quite to the river and where it might cross the highway yet, well, you could still see where the river was by looking off into the distance and seeing that line of trees, and you were most likely to know that there was the river. You could almost even orient yourself along it sometimes, depending on which way the river flowed, how high up you were and how well you could align your map with where you really were.

Well, this guy was saying on the documentary or whatever that there was also this thing where the people up in Canada, well, most of them—a majority of the population, but I don't recall how many—well, they all lived within something like one hundred miles of the border with us down here in the United States. And as it turns out, it isn't because of what you might think—it is not because they want to be near the United States or anything, but rather that it is just a whole hell of a lot warmer the farther south you are, and the closer you are to resources and provisions and such, on account of the roads and transportation and the like. So it is kind of like trees growing along a river.

Well, once again as I sat there and looked out at the trees and thought about this whole thing with the trees and with Canada, I started thinking about how that works in folks' lives. Sometimes we have trees growing in places and they are something like a symbol or a sign of something that allows them to be there. It ain't so much that they want to be there or that we even want them to be there, but they just end up being there because that is where they can be—maybe the only place that they *can* be. Funny how it works like that, and how some things are like trees in that they crop up in our lives not by our choosing but just because there happens to be something in our life that give them the opportunity to be there.

I looked over and Blind Charles had his eyes closed and he was kind of wheezing. I had heard a long time ago that he was asthmatic, and I wondered if being outside along with all of the excitement of the morning had maybe triggered something in him to make it hard to breathe. "You OK?" I asked, breaking the smooth, pretty good-feeling silence.

"Yeah, I'm OK," he said. "I just don't feel too good."

Now, I was going to say something about how swallowing a guy's finger whole might cause anyone to feel kind of sick, but I thought that maybe I should just keep my mouth shut about that. I was really kind of struggling whether or not I should say anything at all, and I wondered what was going on with that old finger. I kind of assumed that the whole idea of reattaching a finger was not all that crazy, but I didn't know what happened to fingers that someone had eaten. I kind of wondered if something like this had ever happened before, and I supposed that it might have but that it couldn't have been all that common. I was going to suggest that Charles put one of his own fingers down his throat and try to get Bitter's finger to come out, but I just couldn't bring myself to say that for one reason or another. As it was I just sat next to him and looked at how sweaty and pale his brow was.

"I only done got sick in public once before, Denny, you know that?" Blind Charles was looking at me just over his glasses, and it was something to look into his eyes without having to look through his thick old glasses. His glasses were kind of an old style, like I said—they had something like big, squarish, tortoiseshell frames that took up an awful lot of his face, and Charles didn't keep them all that clean—they had a lot of dust and smudges and now little drops and smears of sweat as well as some of Bitter's blood on them and that really didn't help their appearance too much—it made them look dirtier than they were and older than they were, too. If you combine all that along with the thick lenses that those glasses had, it was unreal. The lenses had such a strong prescription that they made Charles's eyes look like they were at least twice the size that they really were, and that just gave him an outlandish appearance. I felt bad for him, a little bit, when we were just little kids, as those glasses were about the same then and they made him look awful. Kids, especially boys, can look so geeky and ungainly when they are just in their preteen years and in early adolescence, and most of us probably didn't need any help looking like we were basket cases, if you know what I mean. We all looked like basket cases, mostly—skinny, zitty, with greasy hair and oversized features that hadn't seen fit to even out yet, what with the massive dose of what the school nurse called hormones. We sure as hell didn't need help looking bad, but Blind Charles had that pair of glasses helping down the road to unpopularity and ridicule almost every day of his life. Poor guy.

"We all went to that hog roast over at the Pearsons' farm, and it was right after the prom that one year in school. Do you remember that, Denny?" I confessed that I did, and Charles continued.

"Well, I had been kind of sick for some time, and that you probably don't remember. I had mono when I was in my senior year, and I had been out of school for quite a few weeks. I never remember being sicker either before or since, and it had a whole bunch of ways that I got sick, if you know what I mean. But worst of all, it made me real weak and at times kinda nauseous when I was recovering. I mean, I was almost better by a week or two before the dance, but when the time came for the night itself, I was mostly all better. I felt weak, but not too weak to go, even though my mom thought it was a bad idea.

"So we went over to the Pearsons', and most of the folk came there from the dance, but a few of us who didn't have dates just put on a little better and maybe a little cleaner clothes and we made our way to the Pearsons' just straight from home, seeing as we had no one to pick up or meet. That's what I did—I just got my older brother Bill to drive me over to the Pearsons' before he went out drinking with his friends, and he said he was gonna come by later on in the evening to pick me up and take me home again. I thought that was a mostly pretty good deal, seeing as how I had no other way to get around, I really didn't have any friends who were willing to take me along, and it was too far to walk in nice clothes.

"I figured by the time I got to the party that I really should have stayed home and I didn't know why I came—I never went to any kinds of parties when I was in school, and this hog roast shouldn't have been any different. I got there and mostly stood by myself near where they were roasting the hog, just kind of minding my own business and staring at that dead old hog just getting darker and darker over the fire as it turned around and around on the spit. I imagined that hog talking to me, or maybe singing a song for some reason, and I got to feeling kind of bad for that dead old hog. Where his eyes used to be got to looking the worst, and every now and again I would hear something sizzle or pop, and I could hear it over the sizzling and popping of the fire, so it kind of bothered me. I knew the hog was dead and it couldn't feel anything, but still that hog seemed pretty close to my own size and age, I thought, so I got to feeling just a little bad for it.

"Well, as the evening got on, I was still mostly alone standing there and watching that hog get cooked right up. I was alone except for that one girl I think you probably remember—her name was LeAnn Warner, and she had the really severe overbite. You remember her?" (I told Charles that I did, but I didn't tell him that LeAnn was killed by a drunk driver last spring on a trip to Atlanta—I didn't think it could help things to share that bit of news with him just now).

"I was standing right near LeAnn, and we even talked to one another just a little bit, and we talked about the hog, and I asked her if she ever been to a hog roast before and she said she had and I asked her if she liked hog and she said she did. So we stood and looked at the hog and at the fire and we watched the eyes and the ears on that hog getting to look worse and worse, and the way the skin was stretching real tight and close across the face of that big, dead hog. You know how that hog skin gets all kind of shiny and brown? Well, it looked pretty good, and I normally would have wanted a piece of it like in the worst way, but as I said I was still feeling a little puny and the smell of the hog, well it made me just a little worse."

Blind Charles got a real sad look behind his glasses, and he took them off to wipe his swollen eyes. He drew a handkerchief out of his back pocket and wiped his eyes with one corner and then snapped the hanky out good and sharp and fluffed it a couple of times and then wiped his glasses off, breathing on them real close up in his mouth to get them moist. My father used to do that when I was a child—long before I wore glasses myself, and I always wondered at the way that things fog up and then can get clear again if you don't work quickly. You hold the glass close, you breathe, it fogs up, you wipe. If you don't wipe right away, the moisture goes away, of course, and you have to repeat the process. Now I've come to realize that so much of life is exactly the opposite—things fog up, you work at making them clear, but if you don't do anything or if you don't act fast enough, things just tend to cloud right up again. I wondered if this wasn't what was going on with Charles.

"So that LeAnn, when the pig was all done, she gets herself a plate of it, along with some of the coleslaw that Mrs. Pearson had made. She made the best damn coleslaw around, I always thought. I was thinking to myself that if there was anything that I could really eat a little bit of it would be that coleslaw, on account of I didn't think that I could probably keep down too much of that pork, fine as it smelled. LeAnn loads up a big old plate of that pork and she walks over to me. Can you believe it? She walks over to me. No girl's ever done walked over to me, Denny, to talk to me or even just to ask me what time it was or where the bathroom was or nothing. And here she was, walking over to me, carrying a big old plate of pulled pork.

"That LeAnn Warner wasn't like the most glamorous girl in high school or anything. She had thick glasses, the same as me, and kind of stringy, dark brown hair, but she had the most tender face and eyes. Do you remember that, Denny? Do you? She had such a tender look about her. Her lips were even really kind of pretty, too—kind of sad, but they could smile . . . she could smile real nice with those lips and I was thinking about that as she walked over to me around the hog roast. She was short, kind of, and she walked kind of funny, but I always thought that was a nice thing, you know what I mean?"

I didn't say anything, but just nodded and felt a breeze blowing across the cornfield.

"Well, she came right up to me, Denny. That LeAnn Warner came right up to me. She came up to me and she smiled at me. No girl ever smiled at me, especially like that. You know how sometimes when you're in town and you go for fast food or you go to a place where you have to order something and there is a girl behind the counter taking your order? Well, sometimes they smile at you and sometimes they don't, but even when they do, you know it's just not the same, because it's almost like they just have to say nice things to the customers and smile. But that is really all the nice words or smile I ever got from girls all my life, and then here is that sweet LeAnn Warner just walking over to me with a plate of pulled pork and smiling at me like it's really genuine."

Blind Charles stopped for a moment and looked down at his hands; dirty, grimy and oily hands with little smears of Bitter's blood on them, smeared from the end of that finger that was now digesting right away in Charles's stomach. He turned his hands over a couple of times, inspected the palms, then turned them over and inspected the backs of his hands. He repeated the process and then made tight, meaty fists out of them and then drummed them on his knees a couple of times.

"So, Denny, I tell you, LeAnn walked up and she smiled and I just stood there like a big old fool. I smiled back and I think my mouth was probably hanging right open, like some kind of weirdo. Ever since I was just a real little kid my brother Mike used to catch me doing that—sitting there and staring out into space with my mouth open, and he would walk over and real gently take his index finger and put it on the bottom of my chin and just real slowly and gently close my mouth. 'You don't want to go around catching flies, Charles,' he would say, and I would laugh and he would put his arm around me and maybe hold my head and give me noogies. I used to love that."

"Mike done hung himself, didn't he?"

"Yeah," he replied. He got all silent for a long time and I felt worse than real bad about asking what now seemed like a dumb-ass question at a time when Charles probably didn't need to be reminded of his brother's death. Sometimes I can say real dumb things. After a minute he started in again.

"Well, she came up and I smiled all dumb-like, and LeAnn, she just held that plate of pulled pork out for me. And you know, Denny, did you ever look sometimes at something and you see more than you usually do? Like you look at someone and you see a lot more than you ever thought you might? Well, I looked at LeAnn Warner, and sure enough if it wasn't like time stood still for a bit. And, strange as it was, all the things that I really suppose that people might have found not to be such the best parts of her, well, heck, I found myself crazy about. She had something of a pretty good double chin, but I looked and her skin seemed so soft and warm and that double chin seemed just so natural on her that I thought it was beautiful. And hell, her stringy hair just seemed like the perfect hair for her head and as I looked at it, well, all I could think about was how I wanted to run my fingers through that hair, as it looked so soft and just perfect. And you know, people used to say that she had a big old set of ears, and your average person, well, hell, they ain't got no time at all for an imperfection like that, but on LeAnn Warner, well, you know, they seemed to me to just hold her hair back just perfect, and they held her glasses at just the right angle, and when I looked at her, well, all of it just seemed kinda right."

After Blind Charles said this I realized what a strange expression had come over his face—it was a look that was mixed up somewhere between puppy love and pain and I couldn't tell which one was stronger in the mix. One of those looks like a guy is telling a beautiful, wonderful story about a great artist who was known for the most beautiful and most tender paintings but then who has to go off to war and he's killed or maimed and so when a guy gets to telling the story of the artist's life, well, you get to the end of the story with just a little bit of regret and a little bit of pain. That's the kind of look that Blind Charles had as he told this.

"So you know what happened?" Blind Charles had turned and was looking straight at me.

"No, Charles," I said, "I have no idea. You never told me before."

"Sweet LeAnn Warner walked up to me and held that plate out and said, 'Hungry?' and I looked down at the plate and saw that she must have liked some of that crispy face-parts like a lot of folks do, and I saw both nostrils. I was so woozy and nauseous anyway and I thought like I might pass out. Except I didn't pass out and I wish I had."

"What happened?"

"I threw up. I mean I really threw up. A lot. Everywhere. LeAnn cried out and ran away, dropping her plate of pulled pork and the snout on the ground. Worst up to that point was that I was on my knees, puking my guts out and those two nostrils were on the ground, just staring right back up at me."

"Charles," I said, "that's awful."

"Well, I was so covered with my own puke and no one really was about to help me out, so I just walked on down the lane to the county road to sit and wait for my brother Bill to pick me up. Well, I sat and waited there, silently, just waited for him to come and pick me up. The night kept going on and getting later, and I saw most of the people leave the party. I was sitting down behind some thickets and bushes at the end of the lane, so no one saw me, but it got really late and most of the folk had left and the party had all but grown dark at the Pearsons'. There was still no sight of Bill, though."

"Did he ever show up?"

"No," said Charles, "it got to be probably three or four in the morning, and I realized he must have forgot about me, so I just started walking back home. I was feeling sick and I smelled to high Heaven from all the puke on my clothes, and I was more tired than I ever remember being, but I walked all the way back home. As it turned out, Bill had got drunk out with his friends, just like he had planned to do, they went joyriding around the county roads, and he just plain forgot about me. I got back around daybreak and Mom and Dad were really pissed at me. Nothing was ever said to Bill, and I tried to explain, but I was the one who got grounded for a few weeks. My mom said I never should have gone out when I wasn't feeling good. She kept on saying, 'I told you so.'"

"Charles, that's awful," I said, "I'm so sorry."

"The worst of it was that LeAnn never spoke to me again, and I never did have the courage to tell her the whole story. I've thought now that maybe after all these years and we being all grown-up now that she would probably understand. I've thought I might contact her family and try to locate her and apologize to her—explain to her what happened."

I figured now was not the time to tell Charles the bad news about LeAnn. His story was probably enough for right now.

V

I got to wondering about what to do next. I couldn't sit here all day, and yet I felt that somehow I should keep an eye on Charles, as I wasn't entirely sure that he was all stable. I thought that maybe I could convince him to come with me into town and we could go to the hospital where Bitter was. I thought that if I was lucky I could get to talking to Blind Charles on the way in to town and maybe convince him to apologize to Bitter. Better yet, I was hoping that if we got in there, well, maybe a doctor or someone would know some way of getting that finger out of Charles's stomach, and that even after all the time it had been in there that they might be able to reattach it to Bitter's hand. Well, I didn't have to worry about a doctor trying to get it out. Charles was taking care of that.

As we sat there on the ground, I heard a terrible churning sound and then a sloshing that sounded kind of like a mechanical pump. I turned my head to look at Blind Charles, and I saw that he was turned away from me and bowed down low to the ground. He was almost up on one knee, and his back was heaving up and down. Well, you can probably figure out what he did. He put his finger in there to go after the other finger, and with a mighty wallop of pressure, his stomach gave up Bitter's digit. Charles rolled back and then stood up, retching again a couple of times, and then bending over to put his hands on his knees.

I could barely bring myself to look at the pile of stuff he had brought up, but better sense told me I had better do so. I stood up and went over to where Charles had been sick, and had to kind of cover my mouth and nose to avoid bringing up something just like it. Sure enough, there in a bloodish-colored pile of partially digested food was a little finger. It didn't look too good, especially the part where it had been cut away from Bitter's hand. I took a stick that was laying nearby and kind of prodded and inspected the stump of the finger and I thought that it would take one really good doctor to be able to put something like that back on to someone's hand. Nonetheless, I took my handkerchief out of my back pocket and picked up the finger. I went over to the water spigot nearby and rinsed the thing off, but it still didn't look any better. I wrapped it up in my hanky and then ran the whole thing under the cold water, figuring that I could at least keep it a little cold until we got it to the hospital in town.

"Charles," I called out to him, "that was great—you done real good! You want to go into town with me to get the finger to the doctor?"

Charles just sat there with the back of his hand against his mouth, and he didn't say a word. He was pretty pale and real sweaty, too. I thought he might go back to getting sick, but he just sat there and breathed kind of heavy. He didn't look like he was going to go anywhere anytime soon.

I ran to the house and gave the wrapped-up finger to Mrs. Dempsey. The guys had told the Dempseys what had happened, and Mr. Dempsey just nodded when I told him what it was that I was handing to his wife in that rolled up handkerchief. They both looked at each other, and then Mr. Dempsey took the finger from his wife. "I'll go," he said, and he disappeared into the house. I thanked Mrs. Dempsey and then I closed the screen door behind me and headed down off the porch. Susan Dempsey, their middle daughter, was sitting on the porch swing, doing her nails. She had a bunch of tissue paper or something rolled up and woven between each of her toes and when I started to walk back to Charles, she hopped off the swing and came wobbling toward me on her heels.

"Was that the finger?" she asked quietly.

"Uh huh," I replied. "He puked it up."

Susan wrinkled her nose at that. "I can't figure," she said, "why a guy would eat another guy's finger. Gross." She returned to the porch swing, wobbling on her heels, and sat down. "Gross," she said again.

I wiped my forehead and looked up at the sky. Susan reminded me of that one girl I had known in high school who tried to tell me that people made too much out of everything. Her name was Julie VeldBoom, and she was pretty in a strange sort of way. If you were into really pale girls with broken teeth, you might find her really good looking. Most guys thought she was a little too strange, but I actually thought she was OK. We never dated or nothing, but we did go swimming together in that old marl-bottomed pond once, and we swam out to the raft. We hauled ourselves out of the water and sat down across from one another with our legs stretched out in front of us. The sun felt really good on my cold skin, and I thought that I could have sat there forever until Julie started talking. We got to discussing religion, as it turned out, even though my dad had always told me never to discuss religion or politics with people you wanted to have as friends.

"I believe in a cave god," she said, smoothing the fine hairs on her forearm with a hand wet with pond water, "a god who has us livin' right here in a cave."

This sounded like something I had read about, where that one philosopher a long time ago had something to say about living in a cave and seeing shadows. "Is this like that one philosopher spoke about?" I asked, "with the shadows and all?"

"I think so," she said, "tell me so I can be sure."

I proceeded to tell her about how I thought it had something to do with how life was kind of like all of us living in something like a big old cave, and how all the action took place on the outside.

"Kind of like not living in the big city, and how we just don't get all the action here out in the county," she offered. I said it was kind of like that, I guessed, and I went on.

I told her how it was like that the folks in the cave, well, they didn't have a real good view of things, seeing as how they lived in a cave and all, but the one thing they could see was all the shadows of the things playing around on the cavern wall. Somehow the folks had gotten themselves all chained up to the wall of the cave, and they had their backs to the entrance (don't ask to explain how that's supposed to work—I think you just have to go with it). There was apparently a group of folks outside, too, who had a campfire going, and when anything passed between the fire and the cave, well the folk inside would just get to look at the shadows that things cast onto the wall. So, if a horse walks in front of the fire, well, the folk inside the cave get to see a shadow of a horse, and that's all. And say a combine goes rollin' in front of the fire, well, the folk inside would get the craziest shadow to see, but they would have no idea what the darn thing is or how it works. I told this to Julie, who was just starin' at me, lookin' all kind of confused.

"This is like that antique show on TV, isn't it?" she asked. I had no idea what she was talking about, so I went on explaining it.

I told her that the darndest thing came when some guy breaks free from his chains and creeps out of that cave. Suppose he sees a horse or better yet a combine going by—he doesn't just see the shadow of the thing. And for the first time he sees the thing as it really is and maybe even gets a glimpse at how the thing works. Up to this point he only has his ideas formed by seeing the shadows. Well, this guy goes back to the cave and tells the people there all about what they been missing, and all about the wrong ideas they had in the past about the way things work. Well, I guess this has something to do with the way that those philosophers work, but I always took it to also mean that the only person who sees it all— shadows and horses and combines and everything all together—is God. Ain't that weird?

So I ask Julie VeldBoom if this is what she means by believing in a "cave god." She just looks at me, and gets a strange look on her face.

"No . . ." she says, "it's just that I believe that there's a god who made the cavemen, and we ain't gotta worry about all that science crap."

I decided our conversation was probably going nowhere, excused myself, slipped into the water, and swam to shore.

VI

So I walked back to where Charles had been, except I couldn't find him anywhere around. I called out for him a few times, but he didn't call back. I half figured that he was getting sick again and didn't have any spare words for me, so I stopped calling out so loudly and just started searching around the farmyard. I poked my head into a few of the outbuildings but couldn't find him anywhere. I looked into this one small building with a real low door. The whole of the little thing was made out of logs, like a lot of the buildings at most farms, stuck together with some kind of mud or cement and having an overall sad look—like it had been sitting there for a real long time, waiting for someone to return and that someone never did. I've noticed that sad kind of look in some folks I know—Stacey Ellison, who lost her brand new husband, Josh, was like that. They had been high school sweethearts and had dated for years, it seemed. They finally got married right after they graduated from school and right before Josh went off to basic training for the Army. Josh wound up getting himself killed in that first Gulf War, and so he never came back. Stacey got around to being mostly like she had been before, or at least most of us thought, but she always had this look about her—a look about her eyes and maybe about her forehead that just seemed to show that she was caught in the middle of waiting for someone and that the wait was going to never end. Sometimes when people are passing a plate of something at a big family dinner—maybe a big plate of ham—and someone is waiting for it at the end of the table and that person sees that the ham is getting low and they really want some . . . well, they start to look kind of concerned, like there ain't gonna be any ham by the time it gets down to them. I've felt that way before when I was waiting for the ham or some such thing, and I bet that I even started looking like that—that look in my eyes and in my forehead. Stacey, she had that look like it was no amount of ham that could ever make a person look that way—like she was waiting for something that would never come and leave her feeling empty and hungry the rest of her life, but totally unable to eat.

And that is how that old outbuilding looked. Like it was the littlest and the smallest outbuilding on the farm and that it was always getting the short end of the stick. I was about to poke my head in there and I stopped for just a moment, feeling like I was going to disturb it and cause it some pain, but I shook my head and opened the door with a bit of a shove. The air in there was dry and powdery and there was a little bit of sunlight shining in through the one little glass window, making a shaft of light hanging right there in the dusty air. I held my hand up to touch it, but as soon as my hand got to the shaft of light the sunlight was all over my skin and it felt like I was just becoming one with the dust. Becoming one with the dust was something I had thought about for a long time—ever since I was a little kid and had read some words like "to dust you shall return," and that all came right back to me just then and there as I looked at my hand and wrist and arm in the dusty air and how it all kind of blended together. I said aloud, "Different kind of dust," and my voice sounded thin and small in the dusty air.

I looked beyond my hand and stepped back with a start. There was a chicken hanging there upside down, or at least the remains of a chicken, being as how it was decomposed, dry-rotted away and withered. I could still tell it had been a chicken by its chicken feet, but it was in pretty rough shape, and it didn't really look much like a chicken anymore. When my dad died in the hospital, I got there late and my brother and I went up to the room. "Go in," he said, pushing me toward the door. I walked in and Dad was laying there, with his chin propped up on a rolled-up washcloth, and he didn't really look too much like himself anymore, either. That is what I always think of now when I see someone changed by death, and that was what I saw when I saw that chicken hanging there.

"Stay outta here," came Mr. Dempsey's voice from behind me. I realized I had been there in the outbuilding for longer than I thought and had kind of been daydreaming pretty deeply, so that I didn't even hear him walk up. I spun around to see him and Susan standing there, her with her arms wrapped around herself real tightly. She seemed like her eyes were all wet and she was shaking a little bit, clinging to her dad's side.

"I'm looking for Blind Charles," I said, kind of apologetically.

"I know. It's just he ain't here," said Mr. Dempsey, looking from side to side. "He's round the front. He's dead."

Mr. Dempsey shuffled away with Susan clinging to his side, and I stepped out of the little lonely outbuilding and closed the door. I could still smell the dead chicken dust in my nose as I walked to the front yard of the farmhouse.

VII

Mr. Dempsey sure wasn't lying. Blind Charles was as dead as could be, laying there halfway on the steps going up to the front porch of the farmhouse, and he looked simply awful. In days to come we would find out that it was really all pretty simple—that massive blow that Bitter had landed in Charles's gut was said to have ruptured something or a bunch of things inside that poor guy, and he just bled right out without the blood ever leaving his body. At the time none of us knew what it was that killed him, so there was some speculation.

"Do you think it was the finger that killed him?" asked Susan.

"I can't imagine that could be the case," said Mr. Dempsey, scratching his neck, "I don't think that a finger could kill a man like that."

"Maybe it was some kind of poison on the finger," I offered, not really knowing what to say.

"Hell, they were just baling," said Mr. Dempsey, "I can't see how anything coulda done that from just baling. I think maybe he was just sick in the first place."

"Sick?" asked Mrs. Dempsey.

"A man just don't go 'round swallerin' another man's fingers when he's completely all right. I reckon he had to be a little ill to begin with. You see how big and fat he is. And look at his complexion—he just looks sick."

"Arthur," said Mrs. Dempsey, "the boy's dead—he ain't gonna look healthy."

"Well, all I'm sayin' is that he mighta been sick to begin with," said Mr. Dempsey. "I can't imagine he was poisoned by anything off of my farm."

"Maybe it was a heart attack," said Susan.

"Now that's the most reasonable thing I've heard today," said Mr. Dempsey, "and I bet you're right Susan."

"He's awfully young, Arthur," said Mrs. Dempsey.

"But he's awfully fat and he sure had a hard time breathing," I said, feeling bad about saying it right after I had said it.

"Denny's right, dear. I think maybe it coulda been a heart attack." Mr. Dempsey paused and scratched his neck again. After a moment he stood tall and hiked up his trousers. "Guess I should call The Sheriff."

"Should we call an ambulance, Arthur?" asked Mrs. Dempsey.

"I think he's pretty dead," said Mr. Dempsey. "And I suppose that if we call The Sheriff right away they'll turn around and call the other folks that need to get called. They'll know what to do." He walked up the stairs, giving as wide a berth as possible to Charles's body lying in the midst of them.

I sat down on the steps next to Charles's body, and Susan sat down next to me. Mrs. Dempsey went around the back of the house, presumably to go in the back door and thus avoid having to sidestep the body. I rested my elbows on my knees, and my chin on my hands. Susan took the same pose, except she drew her body tighter together and kind of squirmed up close to me.

"Charles?" I whispered.

There was just the sound of the wind blowing through the trees and a cicada that was trying to buzz its way to a mate.

"Charles?" I whispered again. I said his name again, a little louder, and I shook his arm a little bit. He felt funny when I touched him, and he didn't respond in the least. I knew it was no use, I guess, but it just seemed like I should try something. I sat back and looked out at the yard.

"Is he gonna be a ghost, you figure?" asked Susan, looking down at him. "Is he gonna stick around our front yard forever?"

"No, Susan," I said, "he ain't gonna be a ghost."

"How can you be sure?"

"Susan, you just gotta trust me—he ain't gonna be a ghost. There ain't no such thing as ghosts."

"There are, too," she said, pulling away from me a little bit and speaking in a hushed tone, "I know there are 'cause Stacey Dan-bridge seen one. She was coming home from the filling station out in Owens Township one night with a bag of hush puppies, 'cause they make the best hush puppies anywhere ever, but after it gets dark and they're getting ready to close they sell them for next to nothin'. Stacey had a taste for hush puppies one night and drove out there and got herself some hush puppies and then was headin' home on the rural route just where it goes past the Ford's place. They say there's a grave out there where a soldier was buried without his head on account it was taken off by grapeshot and never found."

"And Stacey saw the ghost of the headless soldier?"

"No. When she got back to Pole Creek she saw a scary old ghost of a horse trying to get into Old Man Thorogood's onion patch."

I didn't say anything about Old Man Thorogood having a snow-white horse that was as old as the hills and that probably for all I knew had a taste for onions. I just nodded. "Well, all the same, Su-san, I wouldn't worry about Charles coming back as a ghost. He's too good-hearted."

"He swallowed Bitter's finger," she reminded me.

"Yeah, but he done puked it up all the same, and he sure felt bad about the whole thing."

We sat there in silence, the three of us. Susan, me, and Blind Charles's most-likely stiffening body. I was always curious about how that thing called rigor mortis works, 'cause I knew sometimes bodies that were dead were soft and limp and other times dead bodies got all stiff. I didn't have any kind of morbid curiosity about these things, mind you, it was more of an honest, scientific curi-osity, and there was part of me that wanted to look at my watch and then start checking Charles, but I thought that Susan might get kind of creeped out. I just sat there and looked at him, and I thought back to that one dream I had about this one girl I was dating a few years ago.

In the dream I walked into some kind of a funeral home, except in the dream it kept switching between a cozy private home and some kind of industrial meat-processing or cutting operation with lots of metal troughs and hooks on chains and pulleys and whatnot. I walked in there and looked down into some kind of coffin that was just like a bed with sides on it, and there was my girlfriend, just lyin' there as dead as a doornail, all pretty, with her long hair falling around her. She was lyin' on her side in the coffin, which I've never seen anywhere else except in my dream, and I looked at her face and noticed that her lips were moving and I could even see her tongue forming words but no sound was coming out. And I went up to the one undertaker who was standing nearby and I told him that she was moving her lips so she must still be alive and how they couldn't bury her and shouldn't they call a doctor?

The undertaker smiled at me and said, "No, the dead just do that. They're condemning us."

That dream stuck with me for a long time, and I thought about that now as I looked at Blind Charles's lips, sitting there, open and kind of puffy. But he wasn't condemning anybody. He's too good-hearted.

◆　◆　◆

I told you a bit about how my dad was when he died, and I told you about the dead crow that Blind Charles saw, and now I went on just a bit about Blind Charles himself being dead, and then I shared my dream with you, so you all know, I guess, a little about how I look at death. I ain't never told anyone about how it is that I feel about death, though, or what I really think the whole point of it is, nor have I ever told anyone about what I think comes next. That probably should be left for another time, but I just want to share something with you.

Strange enough for these parts, a lot of us weren't brought up going to church, like you might expect. In fact, a lot of folk I went to school with, well hell, I don't know if they've ever even been inside of a church or listened to someone pray, let alone sat and listened to a preacher give a sermon—especially a real fire and brimstone sort of thing. Maybe part of that is good, maybe not. I ain't sure. I've done a lot of readin', though, and I have some ideas and a whole lot of questions for someone, if anyone could ever presume to give me any kind of answers. I don't reckon anyone really can, though.

Even though my mom and dad didn't get on me about it, I believe there is a god who made us all, and I get this sneakin' suspicion that he probably has revealed a whole lot more about himself to us than a lot of us think, and maybe less than others do. Whatever the case, he has revealed himself, I really do believe it, but I just ain't sure what it's all about. Whatever or whoever any kind of a god turns out to be, I think he's gonna have to have something to do with mercy and love—I think a god of forgiveness might be the most plausible thing I can imagine, 'cause Heaven knows we sure as hell need lots of forgiveness in this world, and we could sure do with a larger helpin' of love than a whole lot of folk display. Have you noticed that?

It's like the time that I was in grade school and Davey Waller got that fishhook caught in his eye. We were all down by the swimmin' hole near Pole Creek (where the Pole Creek itself widens out and slows on down) Davey wandered up on the shore and went upstream just a little bit—I saw him get out and walk up there and I thought he was walkin' up there to take a piss and I nearly shouted at him to piss downstream, but I didn't want to embarrass him so I kept quiet. Next thing I know I hear him start screamin' like he been bit and we all rushed out of the water and up to where he was. There was Tanner Hadley crouching down to look at Davey who was screamin' bloody murder and holdin' his face while he rolled around on the ground. It seems that Tanner was fishin' just upstream and Davey, like a dumb fool, walked up behind him. Tanner cast out his line and it done caught Davey's eye. It was bad, and in the end Davey ended up losing his sight in that eye and now he always wears an eye patch. The beautiful part of it was that Davey never held anything against Tanner, and he and Tanner became pretty fast friends, even though they was a few years apart in school.

A couple years ago Tanner got really sick with a bad kinda cancer or something—something made all his hair fall out and he got real thin. Tanner didn't have any family to speak of, and Davey and his wife Priscilla took Tanner into their home, caring for him and turning their guest bedroom into kind of a hospital room for him. Davey even sold one of his motorcycles and they got some kind of a hospital bed for Tanner to lay in all day long when he was really ill and weak. When the end came, it was Davey by Tanner's side right to the end. I heard that Tanner at the end kept going on about how he still felt so bad about Davey's eye and how he was more than a brother. Davey buried Tanner in the Waller family plot outside of Haverland, and I ain't never seen a man grieve more for a flesh and blood family member. The shock came when Tanner's estate was settled and every last cent that Tanner was worth went to Davey and Priscilla—it wasn't much, but it was all that he had. Every last cent. Those two went out for each other all the while they knew each other, and even right to death and beyond.

So I think that is how a real god would have to be—ready to give of his love to the end and even right beyond. A god who can forgive, and then show his love to the same ones who might even hurt him, if it is possible to hurt God. Crazy like that, it is.

VIII

The Sheriff came out to the Dempseys' place, and an ambulance that came out slow and quiet, as well as the coroner who drove down from Cotton City and wore a really uncomfortable-looking blazer or sport coat that looked way too small on him. The coroner in the too-small coat looked at Charles and took down some words from Mr. Dempsey and they loaded Charles onto a cart and covered him up with a mint-green sheet that looked like paper of some sort and reminded me of going to the dentist when I was just a young kid. I ain't been to the dentist in years, but I figure my teeth are OK.

They piled Charles into the ambulance and closed the metal doors behind him. The coroner slapped the ambulance and said, "No need to hurry." I thought about that and I realized how true that was, but how it seemed that had almost been Charles's motto throughout life. No need to hurry. Charles used to say that when we was all rushing to get somewhere, and it sometimes kind of held us up, but he would just say, "No need to hurry." It brought us down to earth, I guess.

One of Charles's last acts, of course, was not hurrying to put that finger in his mouth, as he just slowly picked it right up, and then slowly put it in his mouth. He even took his own sweet time about swallowing that finger, and then, when the time was right, he took his own sweet time about bringing it back up again, too. Charles was way too young to die, as far as I was concerned, but he didn't really rush to his death—it was on account of his actions, but it was the doing of another, so you sure can't say that he rushed.

After everyone drove out of sight, I realized that it was just the four of us there at the farm—Mr. and Mrs. Dempsey, Susan, and me. Charles was dead and gone, and everyone else was with Bitter at the hospital. Sure as hell they didn't all need to go on up there, not every last one of them, but I knew and Mr. Dempsey knew as well as anyone that they all were just taking advantage of an opportunity to get out of working at baling on a hot summer day. It was a shame, 'cause we had a lot of work facing us and the weatherman had been saying that we had showers coming. That old saying about "making hay while the sun shines" isn't just a saying for those of us who actually work at making hay.

"Well, you might as well come on up for a spell," Mr. Dempsey said to me, motioning to the chairs on the front porch of the farmhouse, "we can have something cold. We sure as hell ain't gonna get anything done just the two of us."

Truth be known, I had the feeling that Mr. Dempsey was still a little bit shaken by everything that had gone on at his farm today— this sure wasn't your typical day, by any stretch of the imagination, and I had no doubt, even then, that the family would probably remember it for some time to come. There come those days in your life, you've probably noticed, that you seem to be able to remember as clear as the day itself. Your mom or your dad dies. A child is born. You lose your job. A man swallows another man's finger and gets punched in the stomach and killed for it. I never would have guessed to add that last one onto the list until it actually happened, but as I said, even right then I knew that the Dempseys weren't going to forget this day.

Mr. Dempsey and I sat down in two of the wicker chairs while Susan and Mrs. Dempsey disappeared into the farmhouse. Mr. Dempsey lit a cigarette and leaned back.

"Son, I've seen a whole lot of things in my life," he said. "I spent two tours in Vietnam, and I've met a lot of strange folk. I watched a lot of strange folk put a lot of strange things into their bodies, and I had the chance to see a few men die because of it. This is the first time I seen a man die for swallowing a finger." He fell silent and concentrated on smoking his cigarette.

The wind had seemed to really die down and it was heating up quite a bit. This I could tell, even though we were in the shade on the porch. The cicadas were picking up their song and I found that kind of comforting. As though on cue, and as though he knew what I was thinking, Mr. Dempsey spoke of the cicadas.

"That kid died with the sound of cicadas in his ears, did you think of that? I've always loved the sound of cicadas. I read once that it is the loudest insect noise on the planet, but more people than not tend to find the sound of cicadas rather comforting."

"I like cicadas. Their sound, I mean," I said.

"I do too," said Mr. Dempsey. "There was a time, when I was in 'Nam, that I thought I might never hear an American cicada again. I was told there were cicadas over there, but I swear if there were I never heard 'em. I wanted to hear the cicadas like when I was back home here, and I used to lie awake, thinking of the times I would fall asleep on hot summer nights, the cicadas being the only sleeping pill I'd ever need. I wanted to come home and fall asleep on a hot summer night hearing the cicadas."

"Was it bad? Vietnam, I mean?"

Mr. Dempsey got quiet and lit another cigarette. "Everything's bad at times. Some things are just worse." He inhaled long and slow and blew the smoke out through his nose. He looked up just as Mrs. Dempsey and Susan came out of the house.

"Sweet tea?" Mrs. Dempsey said, handing me a tall sweaty glass.

"Thank you, ma'am."

"The Sheriff said he was going to go have a talk with Bitter," said Mr. Dempsey. "I get the feeling this all ain't over yet, despite that kid going away dead in an ambulance."

Mrs. Dempsey drew a pained expression onto her face and got up. She walked to the edge of the porch and looked out at the fields.

Lookin' back on it now, I realize that this was about the first and only time that I ever really heard Mr. Dempsey ever really say anything at all about his time in the Army. Most of us knew that he had been over in Vietnam, and that he had a rough go of it after he came back, but he got his life pretty much all together, so you might never notice that there were things goin' on inside him that he never wanted to let on to. We're all like that in a way, but some guys have a lot more goin' on and Mr. Dempsey and a whole lot like him maybe had more.

I got the impression that Mrs. Dempsey was tired of talking about the affairs of the day, and I reckon Mr. Dempsey got that impression too, 'cause he closed his mouth on the subject and didn't open it again, at least not while I was present. In fact he kept his mouth shut for the rest of my time there that afternoon, aside from the last thing I heard him say that day as we all still sat there on the porch and looked at Mrs. Dempsey lookin' at the fields.

"Rain's comin'. Rains don't care what's on your heart."

◆ ◆ ◆

It stormed and it was a big one. Winds got pretty high, too, but nothin' out of the ordinary, I suppose. It was Pole Creek—the creek itself and not the place—that people remember from that night, but it only gets to be a story when you know it all and know that Bitter came back from the hospital with his hand bandaged up and there bein' no way to put his finger back on.

The winds picked up just after nightfall, and the rains really came on hard. I had left the Dempseys' place later than I thought I would, as I sat on the porch after Mr. and Mrs. Dempsey went inside. I had sat there on the porch and listened to Susan tell me about how she watched things out in the fields when she had free time—she would watch bugs gettin' it on and dead birds getting eaten and she swore she tried to watch an old fallen tree rot.

"You can't watch a tree rot, Susan," I said, "that's like watchin' paint dry, and you just can't do that—it's a figure of speech."

"I seen it, though, I swear, even though it might have been a dream. It was like I watched inside of that old tree and I could feel it giving up. I could feel that old dead tree just didn't have anything else to do except just give in to what was next, and it just wanted in the worst way to go back into the earth. It just felt so sad, like it had disappointed someone and it didn't know why to stick around, nor what for. You know what I mean?"

I confessed that I really didn't.

"You maybe gotta try not to think so much, Denny." Susan hopped off the porch swing and walked past me toward the screen door. "I should go in and get cleaned up. See ya."

She went in the house and I figured that was probably her way of tellin' me that she was done talking and that I could just go home. Well, that's what I did, and I got goin' just ahead of those rains, like I was sayin'. The skies got dark, and the rain came down like it was tryin' to punish someone. I drove down the rural route back towards Haverland, but I pulled over at one point about two miles down the road and just watched it come down, although it was more like I just felt it come down, as I couldn't see a whole lot. I could feel the whole of my car move with the wind and with the rain, and the rain was hittin' and hittin' and hittin' and I got to that point where you are almost convinced that the car is gonna break or snap apart or something—like some kind of structure in the roof of the car or the body or something is going to give way and I would get swept away with the wind and the rain and they wouldn't ever find either me or my car and of course it was all just senseless fear.

After about a fifteen minute wait, sittin' there and listenin' to the wind and the rain and feelin' it blow the car all around I turned the key and started up the engine again. I flicked on the lights and that was when I seen it—the Pole Creek was up over its banks just ahead about twenty-five yards away over the road. Hell, I thought, and put the car in reverse to do a Y turn. I headed back toward the direction of the Dempseys' place, and seen that the creek was up over the banks almost everywhere the road got near it. It took me nearly an hour to get back home, as I had to go south out of the township and it was well dark when I got home. I remember eatin' a sandwich, showerin' off and goin' to bed. The rain and the wind on the roof of my apartment pretty much put me to sleep.

IX

"Bitter done shot himself." Those were the first words I remember hearing when I showed up at the farm the next morning, and I don't remember who said 'em to me. Seems he was back from the hospital in the city, and they told him what happened to Blind Charles and The Sheriff had been by to see him, and Bitter was drinkin' like he usually does, and he got worse'en drunk on account of the pain medicine they gave him. His brother Niles said he got pretty broke up about the whole day and then about Charles and it was just like a big dirty ball that gets to rollin' and rollin' and gettin' bigger and bigger.

Niles heard the gunshot in the middle of the night, and Sheriff came back and Bitter went to the hospital in an ambulance this time. I don't know and I didn't think or care to ask if anyone said, "No need to hurry," and slapped the ambulance door, but I could just bet no one did. It was rainin' and stormin' at Bitter's place as well as it was at mine and everywhere else in the county, so I can only imagine that no time was spared and no words were wasted trying to stay out of the weather. *Damn like hell to shoot yourself on such a stormy night*, I thought.

"Bitter done shot himself." That was all I heard at first, and it was like one time when I was a little kid, and I was watching a story on TV—it was some story about a boy and this rabbit and the rabbit was gonna give this boy some kind of a magic egg that would allow the kid to have any kind of wish that he wanted. This rabbit, of course, didn't look like just any old rabbit—it was bigger than the boy and was wearin' some kind of a vest and a top hat, and he had these big old front teeth that stuck out of his mouth a lot like Corey Dyer's in grade school. Everyone used to kid Corey about his teeth and say mean things to him about those old teeth but eventually they got fixed and Corey didn't get teased anymore. But the rabbit had big old teeth and he gave this magical wish-egg to the boy, and it was just like I knew what the kid was going to do with that old magical wish-egg, because he gave it to his mother or his father or someone, so that they could make a wish instead, and right before he gave the wish away, I said aloud, "He's gonna give that old wish-egg away."

I was right about that rabbit in the vest and top hat and about what the boy was gonna do with the magical wish-egg, and it was just like that when someone said "Bitter done shot himself." I could have almost said it right along like I was readin' it from a page. I didn't feel surprised, and I didn't even feel real sad at first. I just stood there in the farm yard and looked at about the spot where it all took place yesterday. The rains had been hard and there was no trace of any blood on the straw or in the dirt or anywhere, but only the kind of little green bits of small, tiny leaves and bits of twigs that seem to be everywhere and especially on the windshields of parked cars and trucks in the field after a real good, hard rain. Those little bits of fresh green leafy bits were everywhere, and right around where Bitter's finger had come off and Charles done swallowed it.

Blind Charles was dead. Bitter was dead. The rains and the creek had made a mess of the roads, what with logs and branches comin' up everywhere and makin' it hard to drive down some stretches of road. The air smelled really good, though, and it seemed as though that if there was one irony in it all, it was the smell and how bright of a mornin' it was. It was still cool out, but you could tell it was gonna be another scorcher of a day. All the blood was washed away, and so was the pile where Charles had brought up the finger. I walked around a little bit and looked at all the branches down and the mess, generally, that weather can make with life. I thought about the mess, generally, that life makes on its own.

There was a moment that morning, just before I set myself to the work of the day ahead of me, that I stopped and looked at some stalks of grass that got bent over in the wind and in the rain, and I almost kind of felt what it was like to be bent over and have no control in seein' what you're gonna be shown and hearin' what someone might say. I looked real deep and hard at those stalks of grass, and I saw the dew or some lingerin' raindrops on the blade, and I felt, once again, real small, like I coulda curled up and shrunk down and just swum right inside of one of those drops of water, and it would be like a new birth, like bein' washed, like bein' regenerated. Like I would die inside of that drop of water, and something else would be born and I wouldn't have a spot of control over that either, and that whatever that was that was reborn could come up out of that water and everything would be different—everything would be new and perfect and whole, and it would be like all the days of the week were gone past, and it was like another day—like the eighth day of the week and the old week didn't matter anymore. I would come up out of that water drop and things would be fresh and things would be new. Maybe Bitter would have his finger, maybe Charles would be starin' at me all dumb like he usually did, and no one would hate each other or be angry and there wouldn't be no fighting.

Now, I never remember hearin' or readin' about any thinkers or writers who talked like this—I just kinda got some kind of a feeling about it after all that done went on. But I got the sense that it wasn't all that crazy, although I know that nobody ain't gonna get down into a rain drop or a dew drop or any kind of drop of water for that matter. But there was that drop of water just showin' itself to me, and I saw something there that seemed to be a lot more real than a lot of things we been taught in school. I know I wasn't bein' real scientific about it, but there maybe comes a time when it's OK to be a little less scientific. I think maybe when you're lookin' at a rain drop, or maybe when you're listenin' to music or seein' a sunrise, or maybe just listening to a friend laugh, that you realize there might be something else. There was this one philosopher that my teacher told us about in school who was all real mathematical and logical and structured when he was a young man—he done wrote some great book that they always published in two languages any time it was printed, just because it was that great of a book. But as this philosopher got older, it was kinda crazy but he got to thinkin' a little bit more like an artist and started askin' questions more like an artist or like a poet than like a philosopher. Now some would say that it made him less of a good thinker or less of a good philosopher when he started askin' questions that way, but I thought it was pretty OK.

This philosopher who started thinkin' like a poet, I was told he even tried sculpting something out of stone, and the spirit of the artist must have been inside of him, because he sculpted nearly the best thing you can imagine. I thought someone said it was like a statue of a crow or something, but whatever it was, he did a good job on it and no one believed he had done it all by himself and not with the help of some kind of master craftsman. Workin' stuff outta' stone, though, it can be like that. Mr. Switchback, when he was still alive, he used to talk about each one of us bein' like a real rough stone—like you might want to make somethin' out of. Well, as it turns out, he said, we all gotta work real hard on that stone, makin' it from rough to smooth.

Susan Dempsey was standing in the yard, lookin' out at the fields. She turned to me as I walked toward the tool shed.

"I told you about that old dead tree just didn't have anything else to do except just give in to what was next, and just wanted to go back into the earth in the worst way?"

"Sure."

"You suppose," she asked, "that sometimes we don't hear what we need to hear, even if it ain't just a dead old tree?"

I didn't say a word, but walked on to the tool shed.

PART III

A Switchback Tale

I

Layin' there and starin' up at the stars, I felt real small. Then I felt kinda big. But not big in a really big, *fat* sorta way. It was just a big feelin' that went away in just a minute when I started feelin' small again. You feel big when you can't feel where your body ends and the rest of everything begins.

I was layin' there on the great big lawn of the Switchback place, layin' there and just feelin' the cool, damp lawn on my shoulder blades. I'd been out for a walk and I went further than I thought I might have, but I went that far, anyway. Pretty soon I realized I was out near the Switchback place, with its nice white fence and the horses, so I just set myself right down in the grass. I knowed I probably shoulda got up and get goin', but it felt so good to sit there. I smoothed my dress out around me and laid back on the grass, thinking of Peter Switchback all alone inside that big old house, him just sittin' there and readin' his books or writing a story or lookin' through his telescope like I knew he did. I knew he would stand there for hours and look through that telescope on dark nights, making notes in some notebook of his. I knowed this on account of how I would sometimes watch from down the road across the fence. I would see his little red flashlight come on for a second or two and then he would go back to lookin' up at the stars. The same stars I was lookin' at when I was layin' there, so I felt a little closer to him for just a little bit—like we was lookin' at the same things, and even though we was probably havin' different thoughts, I liked the idea of just lookin at the same things, even with him not knowin'.

I'd knowed Peter Switchback from the third grade, I think, and he'd always been the kid in school who done good. Hollerin' I was, that one day, hollerin' at Kevin Maage, that blond-haired kid whose parents were immigrants from some place and they spoke with a funny way about them when you'd see them in the store, when you'd see them at all. Up and down the aisles they'd walk, buyin' the strangest combinations of things. You can sometimes tell a lot about how normal or how weird a person is by the things they buy, you know, and when they buy strange combinations of things, you can tell a whole lot about them. They bought fish—a lot of fish, it was. But Kevin was so blond-haired and had such nice blue eyes that I didn't think about the smell of fish and such on him until that day when Peter Switchback found me hollerin' at him, and me doin' so with good reason. When a boy wants to see what's under a girl's dress it don't matter how blond his hair is or how blue his eyes are when she don't want him to see.

Peter Switchback knew that, and I was hollerin'. And he done took care of me and he done took care of Kevin. And that was a long, long time ago when we was little kids. And this I thought about and dreamt back to and held in my heart and my memory as I was layin' there on the great big lawn of that Switchback place, lookin' up at the stars—maybe just like the stars that he was maybe lookin' at just that very minute not just a couple hundred yards away. And I wasn't a girl anymore, and had I wanted to go talk to Peter Switchback about what was under my dress, I know he still woulda been a gentleman and just asked me if I wanted a ride home or was I not feelin' so good. And I woulda taken a ride home from him, and I woulda burned like crazy sittin' there in the cab of his pickup right next to him, or if I was lucky it'd be in the seat of that fancy little foreign car that he would drive down the lanes and you'd see him on the highway, headin' to the city. Maybe he'd drive me home in that, and I'd be sittin' there and if it were daylight then people would look at us in the pretty little car and my hair would be blowin' as maybe he'd have the top down on it, and people might see us laughin' and they'd think that Peter Switchback was sweet on me, and maybe we had something goin'.

But it was night and I just stayed there, layin' in the cool, wet grass, lookin' up at the stars. And later the lights in that Switchback place went out and I knowed that Peter was in bed and I was gonna walk home. But I knowed his heart was good and so was mine.

Burn, a heart does, sometimes.

◆ ◆ ◆

The trouble was, I didn't go on home. I sat up, and got to kneelin' there in the cool, wet grass, lookin' at that darkened house, knowin' he was inside, all asleep. I bet he was breathin' real slow and deep, and maybe even dreamin'.

Dreams can almost hurt if you ain't in 'em. You know what I mean?

I started thinking that I was in a dream that Peter Switchback was having . . . I tried to imagine bein' in his dream, and we were sittin' at a table outside of some cafe or something in the city—a kinda place I ain't never been, mind you, but I seen it on TV. We were sittin' there and talkin' and laughin', and people knew we were together, 'cause they'd look at us and smile, and when I seen that, my heart just felt so good. Like sometimes how you feel like there ain't no one out there for you and your heart kinda hurts, but then something happens to make it not hurt so bad, and that was how I felt when I thought of myself laughin' with Peter. And I imagined myself taking the ribbon from my hair and putting it around his wrist and he laughed and as I knelt there in the grass, I reached up and took the real ribbon right out of my real hair—this was not in any dream, but I really done it. And I looked at that silky blue ribbon and remembered why I always wore that kind, and it was on account of him. I knew that his favorite color was blue, and he was always in beautiful suits and jackets and even fancy ties most days, and all so often in all different shades of blue—prints and paisleys, solids and whatnot and he just done always looked so good in that so I took to always wearin' a blue ribbon in my hair. The one day he came to the store and as I was helpin' him check out he said he liked my ribbon and I felt my heart race like it was gonna explode and I think I just stood there with my mouth open and he said "Blue . . . for our Lady." I was speechless and I think I said, "Oh," or somethin' and then he looked right through me and said "And it brings out your eyes." He walked out of the store and I think I just about died.

So I had my long, silky blue ribbon in my hands and I knew I wanted to give it to him right then, but I was not on your life gonna do such a thing. But my legs got the best of me and I got up and started walkin' to the house through that cool, wet grass. I didn't know what I was gonna do when I got there, but I guess my heart didn't care too much. I got to the edge of the driveway and something sharp in the gravel hurt my foot and I almost cried out, but I didn't and in another step I was on the blacktop drive—still almost warm from the day. I got to the front door and walked up on the single concrete step and stood there for the longest time, not knowin' what to do.

Part of me wanted to ring that doorbell and wake Peter up, but I knew I couldn't do that, so I just looked at the door. He had the strangest decoration as a knocker—it gave me the creeps, to tell the truth. It was like a crest or a seal or something and it had a pelican on it, with a bunch of words in Latin. I reached up to touch the bird's beak, and I found it smooth and cold and dry, and I saw that the words were all cut out of thin metal and were just attached to the rest of the knocker. I took my long blue ribbon and found a way to drape it over and behind the word *Domine*, and I tied it in a loop. I stepped back and that was when I heard a car comin' down the lane.

I turned to see headlights a few hundred yards off, and I dashed off the porch back to the field where I come from before. I heard the garage door opener start workin' and I knew it was Peter. He hadn't been sleepin' in his bed at all while I was imaginin' us together in a dream—he had been out, and all at once I imagined him out on a date with some girl up in Cotton City or maybe all the way in Birmingham, and I was rushin' through that open field, gettin' all out of breath and not seein' right 'cause my eyes were wet and I was shakin' from fear and my hair was blowin' around. I musta looked half crazy.

I think I ran almost all the way home, and never stopped to go back and look for my shoes, and that was bad 'cause I had done more than just prick myself on somethin' in the edge of his driveway. And if Peter had been in Cotton City that night, well, I got to go too—my roommate Denise drove me to the emergency room and it took a few stitches to close up my foot. I spent the next few days limpin' around the store with my foot wrapped and I was scared to no end, thinkin' I musta bled on Peter's step and he would think I was all crazy and he could put two and two together 'cause he ain't dumb. I thought right.

A box showed up on my porch a couple days later, all wrapped in blue paper, and inside there was a beautiful blue silk scarf and a handwritten note on Peter Switchback's personal stationery.

"*Non sum dignus*. And I hope you heal quickly."

I had no idea what those three words meant, but I collapsed to the kitchen floor and cried like a baby.

◆ ◆ ◆

And that was by no means the beginning nor was it the end of the tale. Sometimes you know a tale or a story all the way through, and you know it so well that when you go to tell it to someone else you almost don't know where it begins or where it ends and you just start tellin' it so that the words come on out. I think that's kind of how it is when I think back to those days when he was alive and I was miserable because I wasn't with him but I dreamed I could have been. Now it's just a whole lot of him being dead and me being miserable because I might have been able to just leave it all in a dream. But there you go.

The tale that I get to thinking about starts with the little bit that I told you, but I think that it mostly plays out in my heart or somewhere like a spirit, if you believe in that sort of thing. A spirit is funny, but only funny in a strange way, so that it makes you think about it in ways that you don't think about anything else. When your heart stops beatin' for all the typical things that a heart might beat for—things like your family, your friends, your dog, your favorite music—and starts beatin' for something or someone else who is relatively new on the scene, it's *then* that sometimes everything else comes to life and you feel for the first time like you really understand all the other stuff. Do you know what I mean? Sometimes I go on a little long, like my brother told me about the way I was talkin' to some of his friends before they went up to Cotton City for that one tractor pull last summer.

And so I've been going on for a little bit longer, already, than I probably should have been, but I have to tell you about how that one particular day ended. The day when I got the beautiful blue silk scarf in the mail.

So I told you that I was sittin' there on the kitchen floor, just kind of cryin' like a baby and realizin' that Peter Switchback knew it was me who had been standin' at his door with a cut foot, bleedin' on his steps and tyin' my hair ribbon around those Latin words on his door knocker. I sat there for a few minutes and just had myself a good cry, cried and cried until the tears just didn't come no more, and then I sat there in silence, listening to the second hand of the electric clock above the stove just make its tic, tic, tic as the seconds ticked by and all that time just slipped right by into the past. My momma used to say something about the seconds and minutes and hours and days and such just slipping right by into weeks and months and years, and how it was just a bunch of one-way traffic from where we were yesterday to where we are today and from here right on to where it is that we are gonna be tomorrow. When momma said it, it didn't seem all that bad of a thing, mostly because we were younger then, and when a person is young, maybe especially a young girl, well, it seems as though tomorrow ain't never gonna get here, and with it the growin' up and the fillin' out and the meetin' the man of your dreams and becoming Mrs. So-and-So and then havin' children and all the things that you think about when you are just a little girl. You know what I mean? Well, when you get a good deal older, things change a little bit and the sound of the clock tickin' on the wall over the stove, well, it doesn't sound quite as good as it used to, and if someone were to tell you that it was the sound of the seconds and minutes and hours and days and such just slipping right by into weeks and months and years, well, it might not sound nearly as good as it used to.

That was the feeling that I suddenly got as I sat there on the kitchen floor, and you might have thought that I would have gotten up and done something a lot more productive than I did—that I might have got up and painted a picture or sculpted a statue or maybe gone across town and got into one of them yoga classes, but that ain't what I done. I just got right up and lightly tied that blue scarf around my neck and I went out into the backyard where there wasn't a soul around just then. And I laid down in the grass and I looked up at the skies, the clear blue skies with the nice white clouds in them and I didn't think of shapes or anything, but rather I just thought of holding myself against the front of a big ball called the earth, and I was on the front edge of this thing—this big old ball—and I was just laying up against it as it sped through the galaxy, and the rush of the wind was holding me fast against it. And I thought these words:

> dashed on rocks and dashed on line after line
> line on line
> line on line
> a blue-dashed world of terror speeds on by
> as fast as the light from a tell-tale lantern
> or a headlight

a pair of headlights
cast the unseen ray of truth and the ray of light that looks like truth

dashed on rocks and dashed on line just fine
a wild torrent
line on line
cut to bleed and cut to the quick
but cut to bleed the way we always said
cut to the quick and bleed on the driveway
dry and hard
and dashed on rocks

I ain't never really written no poetry before and this just come right out. I said it over and over and over again, and when I went in I eventually wrote it down, but I wrote it down while I was in the dark 'cause I laid there in the grass until sundown and past. I started gettin' hungry and that was when I went inside to get some food to eat and write this down, like I said.

I still ain't sure what a lot of the words really mean or quite why I wrote them the way that I did, but it was just like they was inside of me and they had to come out just the way they come out. And the odd thing was that at the time those words didn't mean as much to me as they did a while later or as much as they mean to me now, 'cause those words they mean some things now that they never could have on the night that I first wrote them down.

II

Travis Martin looked at me hobblin' around on my first day back at work and he just stood there givin' me the strangest look. Travis was probably about twelve at the time, and he was always kind of a weird kid—the kid in town who was the last one wearin' shorts in fall and the first one to go talkin' about how aliens were the ones who cut up the cow in Mr. Dempsey's yard that one time. The hell if it was aliens, of course—it was just some kids come down from Cotton City and for some dumb reason (mostly that they were drinkin' but it never much got talked about) they managed to somehow kill a cow and the Sheriff's department passed it off as "criminal damage to property." Well, sure it was property, but it was a cow, too, and killin' a cow is a lot worse than spray paintin' your name or some filthy words on the side of a barn or something. But it wasn't aliens, that's the bottom line. Travis thought it was, though. Dumbass.

He looked at me hobblin' around and he just stood there quiet until he turned away from me and said "Cut yerself?"

"No kidding, Travis," I said, giving him kind of a dirty look and walkin' right past. I didn't want to answer any questions and I didn't want to get to talkin' about what happened.

"Pilly Dawson says there was blood on the sidewalk outside Walker's place." The Walkers were widely known to still make their own booze—Grandpa Walker had been a moonshiner of sorts, and it was said they had the still yet, and what's more they used it. If you asked around, most people who weren't necessarily the kind of people you would spend a lot of time associatin' with would tell you that the Walkers could set you up with a few bottles if you were willin' to pay. The whole county is dry, so no one really talks about it, 'ceptin' for the folk you shouldn't be talkin' to in the first place.

"Pilly says he thinks it was you who cut yerself and then bled on the sidewalk outside of Walker's place. Pilly says you was probably gettin' a bottle." Travis said this and then he walked off real fast and went down the pasta aisle and then out the store. Travis was about as dumb as a rock, and the worst part was that he would believe almost anything you told him, and then he'd go puttin' two and two together, comin' up with five and then goin' and tellin' everyone. As he walked away from me I just said something to him under my breath and I can't rightly remember what it was. I was a combination of hurt and embarrassed and angry and something else that I just couldn't put my finger on. It's a strange combination of feelings, but I had kind of a habit of gettin' strange combinations that way. You know how it is, I bet, and if you don't then you'll find out sometime. Trust me.

That whole day was just kind of bad. I worked a regular shift at the store, and then I went back to my apartment with my foot kinda hurtin' pretty bad, so I decided to take one of them pain killers that the doctor done gave me for it, but that I hadn't really wanted to take on account of how loopy they made me feel. So I took one and then I sat there for a while and I didn't really feel anything different, so I took another. After I changed outta work clothes and into my comfy blue cotton dress, I got out a mostly empty journal that I had been keeping some time ago. I went out to the back porch and looked up at the skies. It looked like it was fixin' to rain, so I thought I could just stay on the porch where I could stay dry. I sat down and spread that journal across my knees and looked up at the sky. I done wrote,

> Peeling halftone half-and-half with a whippoorwill walk

I didn't really know why I had written that down, but it sounded nice when I rolled it over my tongue a couple dozen times, so I continued:

> mazey strutters carry half-tones and wobble all the way
> madcap hullabaloo and a whippy little smile
> makes a haberdasher holy for the basket-trapping latch

I was really kinda confused, but it felt so good to write those words I just didn't want to stop and I thought that if I could write everything that I wanted to ever say then I could somehow make all the feeling go away and all the feeling come back and maybe rearrange all that feeling into some sort of thing like I thought that I should know. You know what I mean? It's like there's a bunch of thoughts about what you want to say, OK? And then you might never say them, and you get to feeling a certain way, but it just confuses you and you feel all kind of weird when you think about it. Well, it seemed as though somehow I could get a handle on all the things that I ever wanted to say and all the things that I ever wanted to show everybody about how I felt, and just kind of rearrange them into something I could work with and something that somebody, maybe, just maybe, could understand. You know what I mean?

and the ghosts pour their tears and fold their hands.

That last part made me sit up and take notice, seein' as how I'm not one to really believe in ghosts and all that kind of stuff. I tried to think about ghosts a little bit but I kind of find it hard to even think about them when I'm tryin' 'cause I just don't know what one would be like or what one would want to do. That is, I don't know what a ghost would want to accomplish. If I were a ghost, I suppose I'd probably want to do all the same things that you thought you might do when you were a little kid and someone asked you what super powers you might like if you could choose—would you want to be able to fly or be invisible or to be able to telepathically communicate with fish or some such nonsense? If I had to combine the best abilities of ghosts and superheroes, I reckon it would have something to do with being able to just fly around anywhere and get wherever you wanted to get in just a minute or two, be invisible and pass right through walls and such. That would just about make me the happiest ghost I could imagine to be. I thought about that, and yeah, I thought about what I would do if I could go and watch Peter Switchback in his big old plantation home, all by himself—watchin' him sleep and watchin' him shower and watchin' him dress, but I thought I would really like to watch him when he's quiet and maybe when he's readin' or writin' like everyone says he does all the time. Sometimes I think you can tell a lot about a person by the way they act when they're all alone, and especially when it's quiet and they are thinkin' and concentratin' real hard.

"Fold your hands and bend your head over the grave
grave thoughts come close and hard."

When I wrote "grave," I stopped and thought about that word— "grave." I reckon it means at least two things that I'm aware of, 'cause it could mean the thing that you put a dead person in—a grave—and it means something like "serious." When I think of the one, my thoughts get like t'other, and it has always been that way.

The one thing that I can never stop thinkin' about when I think of the word "grave" is the day when I was about six or seven years old and my Aunt Celia was gettin' buried at the Haverland cemetery and it seemed for all the life of me that every last single person in the whole danged county had showed up and was gonna be there for the service. If you ever been to a funeral when you was just a little kid, maybe you know exactly what I'm talkin' about. There were foldin' chairs and a whole lot of linoleum and there was this sickening smell of some kind of floral perfume—it was sweet and cloyin' and I didn't think that I would ever want to smell it again after I smelled it the first time. It was something like flowers, but it had this heavy smell that just hung right there in your nose and it never seemed to go away. There was maybe a hint of talcum powder to it, but it was so hot and heavy and I thought that if I was gonna have to sit there and smell it much longer that I would probably just get sick. And there was so much linoleum and it had a smell, too, and then when I lump it all together, it just smells like death. Or maybe I should say it just smells like someone died, but not like the same way like when you say there's somethin' died under the porch.

◆ ◆ ◆

I wrote those words down and I started feeling not so much sleepy as I started feelin' like I had to lie on down. I got up and walked into the middle of the yard and I laid down there in the middle of the grass. I had that same feeling like I had just the day before, when I was feelin' myself held up against the earth while I was lyin' in the green, green grass. Here I was in just about the same place, and in just about the same sorta situation, and I got just about the same sort of feelin'. Ain't that crazy? Well, maybe it ain't all that crazy, as the same sorta circumstances might make you expect the same sorta results, and that's exactly what I got.

I was lyin' there, all kinda spread-eagled like I was before and I started thinkin' about time and the smoky kinda ropes that time makes up when it winds around your life and the way those ropes start windin' in places you don't expect and before you know it whole parts of your life are dragged into the story that your life makes. I had never thought about a person's life bein' like a story—in fact, kind of like a story of the sort that you might read in a book or in a magazine—and a person's life might just kind of get to unfoldin' like that kind of a story when the smoky ropes of time wind on to things and pull them out into the light and out into the middle of the story.

Well, I laid there and I started feelin' myself all light and then I started feelin' all kind of heavy again and kind of like I was dreamin' except I sure wasn't tired. And I saw myself walkin' outside of town down the road to Pole Creek, 'cept I knew I was still lyin' there in my backyard. I was walkin' down that road, though, and the road was changin' and the road was gettin' worse but not bad—it was gettin' to be like an old-time dirt road and things around it started lookin' different. The road signs I expected weren't there but all the smells and things I woulda come to expect were. I could smell the sourwood blossoms before I could see them and the heat rose up off the dirt road to meet me as I walked. And the man in the gray uniform on horseback seemed to be as natural in the landscape as could be.

He rode up alongside me and at first I barely would have thought to look up at him. He was young and handsome and he was wearin' an old gray uniform like you used to see in the history books. Part of me couldn't believe that he was there, but like I said, he seemed to be as natural as could be. He looked down at me, smiled, and then removed his hat and tipped it to me, lettin' his beautiful russet locks spill right out and fall down in front a' him as he bowed to me. Like I knew right then and there what I was doin', I did one a' them curtsies like we was taught in grade school a long time ago and he smiled at me, flipped his hair back behind him and put his hat back on his head.

I walked along with the man on horseback riding just a few feet away from me, and for all the life of me, while I could smell the sourwood and feel the breeze and the heat risin' off the road, I couldn't smell his horse, nor did I feel when he rode up—it was like I was only seein' him on film, except that I knew he was there and as real as could be. I was about ready to stop and reach out to touch him when he spoke.

"Miss, I do believe you're lookin' to reach out and touch me," he said with a strong but gentle voice that spoke something that sounded more like a statement than a question.

"Yessir," I said, catchin' my breath, "I don't mean to be in your way. Sorry."

"You're not in my way at all."

I thought about his voice and he spoke so nice—it seemed he spoke in an old sort of way, such like you don't really hear anymore 'cept maybe in movies. I looked at him again, this time real close and I knew he was a soldier of some kind, but you don't see soldiers on horseback, of course. "Where are you from?" I asked, squintin' one eye closed and wonderin' what kind of answer I would get.

"I'm from right around these parts, Miss. Out near Owens Township to be exact."

I knew there weren't any folks who lived out anywhere near Owens Township except the Fords who had their farm out there, but I wasn't gonna say anything to him on account of how nice and polite he was. And it was then that it struck me that while I was lyin' down in the grass in my backyard and at the same time walkin' down the rural route to Pole Creek that didn't look quite like the way to Pole Creek anymore, well, I was havin' a talk with a man who might not be there or at least was there at one time and might not be anymore. I didn't want to ask, really.

"You must follow, Miss, what is in your heart. Forgive me for asking, but do you know that?"

I wasn't too sure at all what to say, and I just stopped dead in my tracks. He stopped his horse and looked down at me. The sunlight kind of framed him and it hurt my eyes to look up at him on account of how bright it was.

"I think I do," I said, shielding my eyes with my hand.

"For you may at this juncture, and at any future juncture that you may happen upon, be directed by your heart, as we all are. The juncture is yours, though, Miss. The choices are yours."

Our eyes met for a brief moment in time and never was I so overcome by such perfect hazel eyes that were rimmed and touched by such sadness as well and shot through with such a gentle spirit. I was at a loss for words.

"Travel safely, Miss," he said, tipping his hat once again. He turned his horse around and rode toward a trail that led off between the trees. I watched him ride out of sight and after he was gone I still stood there, lookin' in the direction he went and listenin' to the cicadas and feelin' the warm breeze, smellin' the sourwood blossoms and feelin' the heat risin' up off the road.

I looked down. The blacktop road was right there like I remembered it.

III

I got to thinkin' about choices the very next day as I walked or rather kind of hobbled to the diner for a little bit of lunch before my afternoon shift. I was gonna just make a sandwich before I went, but I'd been eatin' at home or out of a brown paper sack almost every day that month, so I was doin' pretty well on not spendin' all my money, and I had a few dollars more'n I usually do in my purse, so I went to the diner, like I said. It was a quiet day on Main Street in Haverland, and when I got inside, it was even quieter yet. I was about the only one there, 'side from Lila at the counter and Henny in his booth. Henny wasn't his real name, but he was drunk near 'most all the time, so no one really took the chance to find it out. That's how he was the day I went in, too—drunk. He was slumped over in his booth and was nodding his head out of time with the music on the radio. It was an old Elvis song that was playin' when I come in.

"Hey Ash," said Lila, and I just raised my hand back at her. I dropped down on a stool at the counter and opened up a menu, even though I already knew pretty much what I wanted. I started flippin' the pages back and forth—both of 'em, as there were only the two pages with one in between, and the food those pages described probably hadn't changed in at least the last fifty years. Only the prices had changed, but then you expect that.

I started readin' the things on the menu, 'specially the sandwiches. Turkey melt. Patty melt. Pulled pork barbecue. Tuna melt. Reuben. Hot ham and cheese. All sandwiches come with chips. Fries are fifty cents more. No shirt, no shoes, no service. And then my eyes landed on it: "BLT."

Now, I ain't never been real big on the BLT, seein' as how it is the bacon, lettuce, and tomato sandwich, and I ain't never been a great big fan of lettuce. My mom was convinced that it was lettuce that used to make me kind of loose when I was a kid, and I'd always have to make a stop at a place that had a restroom. That's probably more information than you really need, but I'll just say that I ain't real big on BLTs ever since I was real young. Anyhow, this day I started lookin' at that menu entry that said "BLT" and I kept readin' that description over and over again: "Crisp fried bacon, garden fresh lettuce and tomato, all dressed with mayo, on toasted white bread." Well that sure sounds good, don't it? Especially that part about the crisp fried bacon—there ain't a single person I know who don't like crisp fried bacon, and mostly I think that any folk will take the limp kind, as well. The toasted white bread sounded so innocent and comforting, to tell the truth, too. White bread, when you toast it, it's one of those things like your momma might make for you when you weren't feeling all that good, and you put that together with crisp fried bacon and you got a meal almost any old time you can imagine. I saw myself ordering a BLT and then I saw Lila bringin' me that big old BLT on a plate with those chips, seein' as how I was pretty frugal and didn't need the fries. I even saw myself picking up that BLT, and I could feel my fingertips on that BLT—the toasted white bread—and then smellin' that bacon as I raised the sandwich up to my mouth—you know how you can always smell bacon before it goes into your mouth?

Well, I sat there ponderin' that BLT for the longest time, and I could just about see myself orderin' one when Mr. Pettigrew (Possey's dad) came in to the diner. Lila was walkin' toward me and asked if I was ready, and when I said, "Not quite," she walked over to Possey's dad.

"Whatcha gonna have t'day, Earl?" asked Lila, pullin' out her pen and pad. "Fried chicken like usual?"

"No, Lila, I think I'm gonna have me a BLT."

"BLT?" asked Lila. "You never have a BLT. What do you want a BLT for?"

"I just been thinkin' of one and can't get it out of my mind. I can have one, can't I?" asked Mr. Pettigrew with a laugh.

"Of course, Earl . . . I might just have to charge you extra for surprisin' me, that's all."

Lila and Mr. Pettigrew shared a laugh as Lila wrote on her pad and then turned to walk my way.

"You decided yet, Ash?"

"Just a tuna melt," I replied. I musta been sittin' there with my mouth open after I ordered, because Lila asked me if I was alright. I told her I was fine and she went to go get our orders put together. I sat there on the stool and just thought about how I had been thinkin' of that BLT like crazy and then Mr. Pettigrew comes in and orders one and then I just can't bring myself to do the same. Ain't that weird? And a BLT was what I wanted most of all just then. Well, I didn't think about it too terribly long, as Henny the drunk over in the corner, started makin' a real bad sound like he was gonna do you-know-what with his lunch or breakfast or whatever it was that he last ate. He hunched right over in his booth and Lila cried out, "Oh no you don't!"

Mr. Pettigrew got up and rushed over and hauled Henny out the door but not before Henny got sick all over Mr. Pettigrew and down the door of the diner. Lila shouted at Henny and Mr. Pettigrew shouted at Henny and Henny just shouted at the sidewalk, except without words, you might say.

Me and Lila was just starin' at Mr. Pettigrew holdin' onto Henny, just kinda' holdin' him up over the sidewalk, and Mr. Pettigrew pulled him right out to the curb and laid him on down.

"Dang if that's what you get for tryin' to help a guy," said Lila. "Earl, I am so sorry 'bout your shirt."

"Damn drunk fool," said Mr. Pettigrew, wiping his hands on his trousers, "Lila, I'm goin' on home—I can't sit around like this."

"That's OK, Earl. You try to do a good turn and look what happens. Thanks for keepin' most of it outta the diner."

Mr. Pettigrew walked off, leaving Henny in a heap on the curb. Lila went back into the kitchen, but reappeared just a minute later.

"Darlin'," she said to me, "I'm sorry, but we're all out of tuna. I hope you ain't in a rush."

I told her I did have to get to work before too long.

"Well, I can put something else together pretty quick for you," she said, "unless you want Earl's BLT. I don't think he's comin' back for it."

◆　◆　◆

Well if that wasn't just the strangest thing, I don't know what was. After I finished my sandwich I went to the store and put in my time, you might say, just thinkin' about what I wanted to do more than anything else. I just wanted to go home and lay down in the grass out back and feel myself holdin' on to the front of the world and see where it took me this time.

It was gonna be a long afternoon, though, and had I known what it was all gonna be like I might have called in sick, even though when I look back on it all now I see that it all had to take place—everything that done happened, well, I guess it done happened for a reason and I sure couldn't have taken any one part of it all and left it out and had it come to the endin' in the very same way. If you don't quite get what I'm talkin' about, that's OK—I think it's a little confusin' if you look at it in parts, and it only seems to make a whole lotta sense when you take the long view, like I was kinda sayin'.

I got to thinkin' about it all like it was a kind of a walk down a path where you had to pick things up in just the right order, and I know you don't really ever have to do anything like this, but you'll just have to go along with me and see what I mean. It would be like you're on some kind of a path through a woods or something, and the first thing that you have the chance to pick up is a basket. The second thing would be maybe a bowl of water and then you have a chance to pick up a goldfish later on. Yeah, I know that's crazy, but if you think about it, it works out just fine. If you picked up the goldfish first, without having the bowl of water to put it into, you almost couldn't do that, now could you? Likewise, you almost gotta pick up that basket first, in order that you can put the other things that you find into it. Well, I think that sometimes in life we go around pickin' things up before we can really handle them, and other times we don't pick up things we might like to on account of how we just don't know that we can. It's kind of sad that way, but I think it's true.

Well, that afternoon there was an old lady that no one seemed to know who come into the store and she just spent the longest time lookin' around for things it seemed like we didn't have—she was askin' for things and we didn't seem to have them. She wanted some bay rum aftershave, something called a "union suit," and some kind of pills she said were for your liver. It was strange.

Well, just after this old lady checked out I went on over and said to her, "Have a nice day," and she turned and looked at me so odd that I started feelin' funny right down in the pit of my stomach. And then she turned to me and started talkin'. I remember most of it like it was yesterday, and that might be because I went home and wrote down as much of it as I could right after she done said it. She spoke with a real flat, dry voice.

"Times was hard," she said, "and I know they don't get to rearin' up and tellin' others the way that those of us ourselves do if'n when people ask, but I know they were hard—harder than most any people ever imagined, and my darling John was the last one that I ever imagined would succumb to the terrors of that fateful age. They called it the flu and I coulda cared a'less if they done called it the second coming or if they had done called it the wisdom of all the ages. I really don't care too much a'tall, but I do just know that my dear John succumbed to those terrors and to that dry, smoky existence in that world with the men on the dry cotton beds, then I just knew the end was near, but the end took nearly a century to come around. Funny how the end takes its own sweet time in getting around to playin' out its life and its lovin' and its end. Funny, but in the end it really ain't all that funny at all. I reckon it's a whole lot more like tragedy than comedy."

The elderly lady grew silent and slumped down on the bench that is right past the checkout counters. She dropped down into the bench and sat there, looking straight dead ahead, with eyes that were already, I suppose, looking into eternity. She let out a long breath that almost all of us in the checkout area heard, and then, without any warning, dropped both of the paper shopping bags that she was clutching. A jar of applesauce shattered as it spilled out of one of the bags. A can of peas rolled out, across the floor, and under the checkout counter where Stacey was working. It bumped her foot and she looked down and then across at the lady.

"Hey, it looks like that lady done passed out," said Stacey.

We all crowded around her and looked close to see if she was breathing. I reached down and shook her arm a little. There was no response, and the arm felt a little funny.

"I think she might be dead," said Michael Rawlings, the bagboy, and I think almost all of us were inclined to agree with him. She didn't look too good to begin with, while she was alert and talkin', and now she looked even worse. I saw that Stacey had already run to the office and was on the phone. A bunch of people kind of bunched around and Michael said, "Maybe we oughta give her some air," and tried to get people to go back to their shoppin'. I just sat there with the lady until an ambulance came, which was quite some time— Mr. Watkins from out on the rural route has an ambulance that he maintains and operates if there's a real emergency and someone has to get up to Cotton City. They been doin' this since that guy lost his finger out on Dempsey's farm some years back.

After they done took her away I finished out my shift and then made my way back home. When I got there Denise was sittin' in the front room watchin' TV and eatin' a bowl of popcorn that she had made.

"How you doin', Ash?" she asked through a mouthful of popcorn.

I told her my foot was sore and still kind of throbbin' and I told her all about the day at the store with the elderly lady talkin' to me all strange and then passin' out and gettin' hauled away by an ambulance.

"Sounds like your day was more interesting than mine," she said, "all I did was dream about a day that never did come."

"How's that?" I asked.

"I ain't sure," she said, "but I know that I did a lot of daydreamin', and I thought about a time when I might get married and move into a nice big house outside of town. And I made myself a BLT for lunch."

This was just a little bit more than I could handle just then, so I told Denise I was gonna take a nice hot shower and then maybe do some readin'. And that's exactly what I did—I stood under that hot shower probably a lot longer than I should have, as my fingers got all kind of pruny lookin'. I had this one special waterproof dressing that I put on my foot where it was stitched up, and I kept it out of the stream of the water as much as I could. All the same, it felt even better to get out of the shower, dried off, dressed, and sittin' down with my foot propped up. I didn't too much feel like goin' out back and seein' if I could go for a ride on the earth that night. I was too tired, and I could still hear that elderly lady sayin' that it's funny how the end takes its own sweet time in getting around to playing out its life and its lovin' and its end. I had no idea what she meant, but I was gonna find out.

I was awfully tired and just ready to be doin' nothin', but rather than doin' nothin' I sat down on my bed and got out my pad of paper and a pen. I just started writin' down the words as they came into my head, and it started somethin' like this:

> Grease-hot burn a chicken skin neck-fold
> and grease-hot like a burning sun,
> burning hot and pinched

I wrote this, I guess, about that lady and the skin that was hangin' from her neck in front—it reminded me a little bit of chicken skin. My grandma had been like that, only when it's on your grandma you don't mind it nearly so much.

> Turn it on and let it play
> turn the dial turn the corner turn the age
> age and age into tomorrow
> tomorrow holds a burning chicken skin
> for me

I suppose this had something to do with how the lady just started talking once she opened up—it was like turning a dial and lettin' a radio station just play and play and play. After I wrote that, I started thinkin' about how it is that if we're lucky we all end up in the same boat as that elderly lady, only we get there not thinkin' that we're all that very lucky at all.

> And the dial is fine and the dial is muted
> but the age lets the music play
> and a grease-hot burn is never so bad
> as a dial that doesnt get turned
> and a song that doesn't get sung
> and a muted mouth,
> muted with a cone of fear and a cone of self-doubt
> old muted mouth
> warbles and warbles
> as the dial fine-dial
> turns the corner on a grease-hot burn
> tomorrow

I'm still tryin' to figure out exactly why I wrote all that last stuff exactly the way that I wrote it, but it sure felt good to get it out.

IV

The next mornin' I didn't have to go in to work, but I woke up kind of early anyway, and as soon as I boiled some water for instant coffee I limped outside and sat down on the porch. I sipped for a while at my cup and watched the sun on the grass; I watched the changin' patterns made by the leaves in the trees and the way the light filtered through them. Sometimes it looked like they were formin' words, and sometimes it didn't—but there were gonna be words then the words were gonna speak to me, I just knew it. I didn't have to wait long.

As I sipped my coffee, I first saw the light come through the leaves and I could swear it looked like the word "be." I thought about that for a little while, and I remember that thing we read back in school where in that play there were the words "to be or not to be." While I never really understood the whole of the play or whatever it was that we were reading, I sure understood something of that word "be," as I always had a lot of thinkin' to do about the idea of just being—the idea of just existin', if you know what I mean. And so when I saw this word "be" lookin' like it was formed out of light in the shadows of the leaves of a tree, right there on the grass in my backyard, well, it all hit me, more or less.

I don't know if I was to take it as a command, or if I was to take it as maybe even a question, but I took it all the same. Being is a funny thing, because I think we're all "being" in some way; that is, some folks more, some folks less, but all "being," if you know what I mean. We all live and breathe and everything like that, but some folks just sit around a lot, and others do a whole lot of things. While I was still just sittin' here, not doin' a whole lot, I decided to keep on looking at those shadows that the sun and the leaves were throwin' off for me to see.

I took another sip of coffee and I kept lookin', until it looked like I saw the word "he." Now that may seem like it looks a lot like the word "be," but it was in a different spot, I'm most pretty sure. It looked a lot like it said "he," and I'll take it for that. The first thing that came to mind was, of course, Mr. Peter Switchback. He was about the only "he" in my mind, and maybe the only one that's really gonna take up the largest part of my mind and my heart if you want the truth, but you probably already figured that out for yourself. The trees and the leaves and the sun and the light, they all got together and they put Peter Switchback in my thoughts almost first thing that morning.

That was about it for words on the lawn, probably as much because of me not lookin' as it was of them not spellin' anything. I thought about "be" and I thought about "he," and it made me go forth between feelin' sad and feelin' warm and nervous. I drank down the last of my coffee and I went and hobbled out into the middle of the backyard. The grass still felt really wet from the dew, so I knew that I'd soak my PJs right through if I laid down in it, but I laid down anyway. Yeah, it was wet, but it felt OK on my back, and I just wiggled myself right down into a comfy spot in a comfy way.

I looked up at the mornin' skies and it was breathtakin'. Blue like crazy. There were some words that popped right into my head as I laid there, and I wrote them down (as much as I could remember) when I got back inside later.

> Water blue and thin like air
> as air is what it is
> air like I breathe
> air like you breathe
> between us, air
> the breath we share

And then I was hangin' on for dear life, I mean to tell you. I had my arms and legs spread out like I was a starfish, and the big old earth was pushin' me along through the atmosphere and the sky and the clouds were comin' along for the ride as we sped through outer space. I knew it was outer space at that moment, even though the skies were blue and it looked for all the world like home. Yet I knew we was movin' right through the universe. And I tried to roll my head from side to side and I just couldn't.

I think I closed my eyes, 'cause that was the only way I could move. I could blink and not much more, so I just closed my eyes for a minute, I think. When I opened them again, the trees were in the same place and everything was the same, as far as I could tell. The earth wasn't movin' no more, and I didn't feel like I was holdin' on for dear life. I tried raisin' my hand and arm, and sure enough they came right up as easy as could be. I sat up a little bit and leaned on my elbows. And then it happened. I thought about gettin' up and goin' into the house for another coffee, and then I thought against it, and it was then that I felt like I split apart or something. I got up and went into the house and I stayed there propped up on my elbows, and everything got real slow for a second. I knew that I would be able to go and follow one or the other or both as I saw fit, so I stayed there, propped up on my elbows, but I watched where I was goin'. Sure enough I just went right in the house and made another coffee.

I stayed right there and felt the mornin' air kind of heatin' right up a little bit. Not a whole lot, but enough to feel good. I thought I heard my name bein' called, like an old man was sayin', "Ashley, Ashley," but I strained to hear and it wasn't there anymore. Pretty soon I was aware of myself comin' back outside and it seemed as though that while I was still sittin' here in the grass, I was walkin' out of the house and makin' a decision about whether to come and sit right back down where I was or if I should stay on the porch and let the mornin' air dry out my PJs. I was aware of the result of only the one I was thinkin' about, though, and I came and sat right back where I was, as strange as that sounds.

My head told me to go and get ready for the day—to shower and get dressed and to have some breakfast. My heart told me to do other things and something that was me just decided to lie right back down in the grass. And my heart got me up and limped right over to the garage and there, right there in my PJs and my hair all kind of flat and stringy lookin' from sleepin' on it, right there I hit the door opener and got into my car. The floor mat was kind of gross and sticky from where I had spilled a coffee yesterday, but I really didn't seem to be able to care. I put it into reverse and backed out of the garage, hardly even lookin' to see if the neighbor kids were in the driveway.

I pulled out on the street and then headed out toward the rural route. I rolled down the window and let the wind blow through my hair, but while I could swear I felt the wind, it seemed as though my hair stayed right in place. That was a shame, 'cause I was thinkin' I needed to do somethin' with it, and a good blowin' from wind would have been as good as anything at that point.

The couple of streets headin' out of town were really empty and at points it looked almost like things were in black and white, alternating with technicolor, if you know what I mean. Like it was a color movie and someone was messin' around with it—turnin' the color to black and white every now and again. It wasn't like it stayed black and white, mind you—it just seemed like for a split second it would be devoid of color and I would be aware of myself just sittin' in the grass, propped up on my elbows. The pea fields and the corn and the trees and the fences and the kudzu just rolled on and flew right by. I was drivin' the speed limit, but my car felt at times like it was standin' still and everything else was movin' past me. Wind that was blastin' against me without my hair blowin' around, trees and fenceposts whippin' by without makin' a sound.

◆ ◆ ◆

The road to the Switchback place wasn't that long, but it took what seemed like ages to get there. For the life of me I could swear that at almost every turn in the road, and at every driveway, and every crossroads I found myself ponderin' what could be and what I wanted to be and what probably could never be. And I felt as though the car was almost floatin' at times, like it was almost on air and that there wasn't anywhere that I couldn't go—like I coulda driven that car right to the moon had I wanted to, or like I coulda made a right turn or a left turn and shot right through the fence lines and skimmed like a bird over one of them pea fields and the trees or nothin' ever woulda touched me and I'd be free like a spirit bird like I felt I was. Damn, but it felt good.

It seemed like forever to Peter Switchback's estate, but I got there and I pulled into that long, long driveway that kinda snakes its way around the house and makes a long approach from one side. It was probably only ten in the morning by this point and I didn't even know that I'd find him home, but sure enough I could see him from the last turn of the driveway. He was sitting in the little gazebo off the side of the house and it looked like he was working on something.

I pulled up to the house and parked, and I got out of my car feeling like I was on some kind of pain medicine, almost. I felt like I was ten feet off the ground, and I didn't even feel like I needed to hobble or limp as there wasn't a bit of pain in my foot. I walked past the front step and that strange door knocker and I even looked down to see if my blood was still there, which it wasn't. I followed the pathway all around to the side of the house, and as I got past the flowerin' dogwood, I saw him sittin' there in the gazebo, talkin' on his cell phone and typin' on his laptop. He looked up at me with a pretty surprised look, but he smiled, and my heart just stopped and then leaped right outta my throat, I mean to tell you.

I heard Peter say "OK, I'll call you later," and touch his phone. He stood up, smiled, and kinda cocked his head a little and just said, "Miss Ashley." I coulda died.

I walked up to him and I didn't know what I was doin' and I suddenly felt all kinda dumb standin' there still in my PJs this late in the morning. He noticed that, of course. "You're into that driving around in your pajamas thing, too?" he asked. I laughed and I think I almost cried.

And I walked up to him, out of my mind and not knowin' what I was doin', and I grabbed his pretty silk tie and I got up on my tiptoes and I kissed him, and he put his arms around me to lift me up to him and I coulda felt our hearts poundin' outta our chests right together. And I mean to tell you I was lost as I never been lost before in my life, but at the same time I was found. I felt our lips together and it was hot and moist and perfectly minty-sweet and I didn't ever want it to end, I mean to tell you.

I don't even know what I said, if I said anything, as I started cryin' so much and he held me and I just was shakin' and cryin' and he held on to me and said he was never gonna let me go and I said I would never let go a' him and would he hold me forever? And he said he would and I was just dyin' and could hardly breathe. And the thing I felt was my heart just burning right up as he held me and I knew that his heart had to be burnin' just the very same way. I knew it, I knew it, I knew it.

Burn, a heart does, sometimes.

The morning passed us by right there on the gazebo. We sat on a wicker love seat with a big white cushion. I curled right up, sittin' on my legs, and I rested my head on his chest. He had some kind of jazz playin'—music that I since have learned to love, and he told me it was by a man called "Duke." Peter held me and we talked about the strangest things, but it was all like I imagined the best kind of dream should be. Soft, dry, warm, safe. With a strong man holding onto you. Ain't nothin' wrong with that.

For the second time that day there were words that crept right into my mind without me really doin' anything about them, and like before I found these were words that just kind of burned themselves right into my brain and into my memory and probably would never dare to leave.

> Dropped and dropped and dropped
> like a potion of hope
> and a drug of love
> my heart-vein holy-hopeness of heavy, heavy load
> drained to weak and weaker
> weakest drain of knee-strength
> saved for kneeling
> and praying
> and praying
> and yelling at a god who finally hears and knows
> he knows what I need
> I need this hope and this holy-hopeness of heavy, heavy load
> potion of hope

drug of love

the same old cliché

never bites or sucks or rolls its tongue around and softens with the

softest word.

softest word

I thought my heart was gonna damn explode or burst and dry up and blow right away. I'm sorry to use language like that, but I mean to tell you it was like nothin' I ever known before, and there weren't a whole lot of words that I could think about that were gonna let me say what I felt that day curled up in my PJs on a soft white cushion on a wicker love seat in the gazebo behind the Switchback house with my head against Peter Switchback's chest and with Peter Switchback tellin' me he would hold me forever.

I told him I had always loved him.

He told me he had always loved me, too.

I told him I wanted to be at his side forever.

He told me he wanted me to live right here on this beautiful old plantation all the rest of the days of my life. He told me there was no one else he would ever say that to.

I reached my lips up to his again. He kissed me ever so softly, and it felt like it lasted forever.

I wish it would have.

V

The sourwoods had the same smell as they always did. The sky was blue, the roads went on to wherever they went. My foot healed up just perfect and normal pretty quickly, thank God. When Peter's friends from his church got done movin' me into the house, they left a lot of food already made, and I almost felt like a widow when folks bring food 'round the house. Yet I wasn't any widow. Not in this world, I guess.

It all worked out the same as I would have chosen aside from one thing. Yeah, *that* one thing. Strange, it is, just like when you are travelin' and you can choose one route or you can choose another and the both of them will get you to the same place, and maybe even at about the same time.

I think the man on the horse was part of the same kind of journey such as I was makin' for a short while. We both were travelin' and followin' different paths. When I caught up with myself I was just about to experience the greatest loss I ever did know, 'cept it wasn't a loss in the typical way. No one gave me condolences, no one sent me flowers, my name wasn't mentioned in any obituary.

While the time that I spent with my beloved Peter was the most wonderful I've ever known, it is not the only memory that I have, for as I said, I caught up with myself eventually, and the world I live in now has a very different past—a past where I was just the girl at the grocery store, where I was someone just wanderin' from place to place and from day to day.

It came like a dream and it passed like a dream but much, much more than a dream, for it was real. And here I was, with nothing really different. It had to be of my own choosing to find myself having come full circle, but perhaps the change and the circling were urged by vapors that knew better and were keeping me from even worse heartbreak. "I want you to live right here at the estate all the days of your life," he said to me in a different place, in a different layer.

And so I shall.

The whole of the Switchback estate, minus some acreage for a riding ranch for kids had been left to me. I was floored, and yet I somehow knew nothing different could ever happen. He had made provision for a lot of folks in his will, but everyone was shocked that I wound up as his chief beneficiary. I think a lot of folk still think that we had something going on behind everyone's back, but they'd be surprised to know how far behind it would have to be.

And so everything is as he had wanted it. I am here, and here I intend to stay. I'm finding a lot of things he wrote, and I'm answerin' a lot of emails and letters. He left a whole lot of stuff for me to do, just in case, as though he knew the end was comin', and something in me can't help but think that's exactly how it was. I take long walks with his dog. I've got his garden lookin' really good. I sleep in his bed, and I have all his things in perfect shape.

And I cry myself to sleep 'most every night.

If only one thing could be different, you know what it would be. I saved what they wrote about him in the paper, but I typed up another version of it that I keep on his writing desk and on my dressing table. I read it every morning, and I read it every night. I read it when I sit down with his mail and when I look at a picture of him in his Navy uniform that I found and had framed and that I put on the desk.

HAVERLAND—MR. PETER SWITCHBACK, Jr., 43, of rural Crawford County, died at 11:51 a.m. Monday, July 12.

He was born in Haverland to Peter Switchback and Ruth Mae Blair Switchback, and is survived by his wife, Mrs. Ashley (Porter) Switchback of Haverland, and a brother, David, of Pole Creek.

He was preceded in death by a sister, Lily.

Peter proudly served eight years in the U.S. Navy on several ships and coastal installations and was most recently self-employed as a writer and consultant and maintained his family's plantation and estate.

He was a life-long Christian and attended St. Alban's Anglican Church in Cotton City, although he charitably supported all of the churches of Crawford County.

Funeral services will be at 2 p.m. Thursday, July 15, at St. Alban's Anglican Church with Father Michael Stencil officiating. There will be no visitation. Burial will be in Memorial Park Cemetery. Military honors will be provided by the Custis Hewitt American Legion Post 285.

Mrs. Switchback asks that memorials be made to the St. Alban's Endowment Fund, the Guild of Mary, or to a charity of the donor's choice.

The Poems from Ashley's Pen

GALAXY-ROT

dashed on rocks and dashed on line after line
line on line
line on line
a blue dashed world of terror speeds on by
as fast as the light from a tell-tale lantern
or a headlight
a pair of headlights
cast the unseen ray of truth and the ray of light that looks like truth

dashed on rocks and dashed on line just fine
a wild torrent
line on line
cut to bleed and cut to the quick
but cut to bleed the way we always said
cut to the quick and bleed on the driveway
dry and hard
and dashed on rocks

GHOST

Peeling halftone half-and-half with a whippoorwill walk
mazey strutters carry half-tones and wobble all the way
madcap hullabaloo and a whippy little smile
makes a haberdasher holy for the basket-trapping latch
and the ghosts pour their tears and fold their hands.
Fold your hands and bend your head over the grave
grave thoughts come close and hard
and tears never come
if the ghost holds forth
and the libelous superhero
hangs his head and wishes he were a ghost

CHICKEN LADY

Grease-hot burn a chicken skin neck-fold
and grease-hot like a burning sun,
burning hot and pinched

Turn it on and let it play
turn the dial turn the corner turn the age
age and age into tomorrow
tomorrow holds a burning chicken skin
for me

And the dial is fine and the dial is muted
but the age lets the music play

and a grease-hot burn is never so bad
as a dial that doesn't get turned
and a song that doesn't get sung
and a muted mouth,
muted with a cone of fear and a cone of self-doubt
old muted mouth
warbles and warbles
as the dial fine-dial
turns the corner on a grease-hot burn
tomorrow

SOFTEST WORD—YOU KNOW IT

Dropped and dropped and dropped
like a potion of hope
and a drug of love
my heart-vein holy-hopeness of heavy, heavy load
drained to weak and weaker
weakest drain of knee-strength
saved for kneeling
and praying
and praying
and yelling at a god who finally hears and knows
he knows what I need
I need this hope and this holy-hopeness of heavy, heavy load
potion of hope
drug of love
the same old cliché
never bites or sucks or rolls its tongue around and softens with the
softest word.

softest word